"Next Satur~~day,~~

"For what?"

"Our wedding."

My throat constricts. "That soon?"

"Take advantage of the good press, start the countdown on our contract."

"And make sure I don't change my mind?"

"A consideration, yes."

I look away. It's all moving so fast. Just like last time. One day, I woke up happy, content. In the span of a couple of hours, I lost everything. My friends, the relationship I had with my adoptive father, my beliefs about the world. Everything, gone in an instant.

But I remind myself, Liam isn't Dexter. This arrangement is different. I'd be a fool not to take advantage of it. Maybe, just maybe, it'll change not only the public's perception of me but the people at the foundation. Maybe, after all this is through, I'll at least have some of what I've dreamed.

WED FOR THE HEADLINES

EMMY GRAYSON

PRESENTS

MIX
Paper | Supporting responsible forestry
FSC® C021394
www.fsc.org

Harlequin®
PRESENTS™

Recycling programs for this product may not exist in your area.

ISBN-13: 978-1-335-21364-8

Wed for the Headlines

Harlequin Enterprises ULC
22 Adelaide St. West, 41st Floor
Toronto, Ontario M5H 4E3, Canada
www.Harlequin.com

HarperCollins Publishers
Macken House, 39/40 Mayor Street Upper,
Dublin 1, D01 C9W8, Ireland
www.HarperCollins.com

Printed in Lithuania

When **Emmy Grayson** came across her mother's copy of *A Rose in Winter* by Kathleen E. Woodiwiss, she snuck it into her room and promptly fell in love with romance. Over twenty years later, Harlequin Presents made her dream come true by offering her a contract for her first book. When she isn't writing, she's chasing her kids, attempting to garden or carving out a little time on her front porch with her own romance hero.

Visit the Author Profile page at Harlequin.com for more titles.

To Dad, thanks for picking Iceland.
Trip of a lifetime.

To Little Man, thanks for encouraging me
to jump into the lake. Worth it.

To Mom, John, Kels and Jim,
thanks for making it possible.

CHAPTER ONE

Aislinn

MY HUSBAND'S FUNERAL is crowded. Not with people who loved him or genuinely miss him, but with Washington, DC's elite, politicians and bankers and investors who have shown up to supposedly pay their respects as they all play the same game of pretending they care.

Just like Dexter would have wanted.

I shake someone's hand, listen to their lies about what a great man Dexter was. I bite back the bitter words that clog my throat and simply nod. Hopefully most will chalk it up as grief or at least have the decency to pretend like this is a normal funeral.

Pretend like most of us in this room aren't glad Dexter is dead.

I can feel them watching me. Once upon a time I would have felt the weight of every curious gaze, every suspicious glance and pitying smile. Would have been thinking of the newspapers' lurid headlines speculating if Dexter Simpson's wife, a woman nearly half his age who married him in a whirlwind romance just months before his unexpected death, had a hand in his demise.

Now, I feel nothing. Just emptiness. An emptiness that has helped me survive the past ten months since Dexter slithered into my life. Ten months since I had to cut the two people I loved most in this world out of my life.

Tears finally prick my eyes. Diana has texted me faithfully once a week. I hope one day I can tell her how much those texts have meant to me, gotten me through some of the worst days of my life.

And Liam…

My heart twists, tightens. I can't think of Liam. I owe Dexter nothing. But thinking about my friend I've been secretly in love with since I was seventeen while greeting people at my husband's funeral is a low I have no desire to sink to.

A couple moves forward in the endless line, older and dressed in black couture. They tell me how sorry they are. Out of the corner of my eye, I see my parents hovering.

Adoptive parents, I remind myself. Dexter threatened to destroy Liam and Diana's careers if I didn't sever our friendship. But he wanted my parents as close as possible. He couldn't exploit his familial connection to a US senator if I didn't maintain a relationship with my family.

I did think of them as family once. Thought I was the luckiest girl in the world to be adopted just before I aged out of foster care, and by a renowned politician and his wife no less. A fairy tale come true. I thought the man I called "father" was different. A politician of integrity, working toward a better world for the people he served.

God, I was so naive.

Senator Eric Knightley is no saint. He has secrets, dark ones Dexter collected and held over my head all the way to the altar. Given how involved his wife, Stephanie, has been in his campaign, including managing donations, I can't imagine a scenario where she's not at least partially aware of what Eric did to secure his office.

I'm consciously trying not to wipe the palms of my hands on my pants when I hear it. That deep, melodious rumble I've imagined so many times whispering words of love to me. Not the sisterly affection he's shown me for the past eleven years, but passionate words, a declaration that he feels the same way I do.

Out of the corner of my eye I see him. Tall, handsome as sin in a tailored black suit, his face comprised of sharp angles and lines that border on beautiful. When he turns on the charm, which is often, his smile is big and bright. But on the rare occasion I've seen him angry, the cut of his cheekbones and the slash of his jaw can go from sculpted to menacing in an instant.

If I would have told Liam that Dexter blackmailed me into marriage, he would have moved heaven and earth to help me. But I couldn't risk Dexter making good on his threats. He wouldn't have just revealed my adoptive father's secrets. He would have destroyed Liam and Diana, too, simply because he could.

The line shifts, and I see Diana is next to him. A different kind of ache takes hold. I may have developed other friendships over the years, but Diana will always be my first and truest friend. She's trusted me with her deepest secrets over the years, as I have mine with her.

Well, all but one. I don't want my feelings for Liam to ever come between Diana and me. And I know, with how deeply she cares for both of us, she would be caught between knowing Liam never wants to settle down and my love for him. Even if he saw me as more than a sister, he's made it clear he has no interest in ever settling down. I would love to have a life with him, but I want my future to include marriage. Kids. Even now, after everything that's happened, a part of me still clings to the slim hope that those dreams are still possible.

I push that aside. I accepted long ago that Liam and I would never be. I still have his friendship, and Diana's, even after ignoring them for months on end. I'm not out of the woods yet. Dexter may be dead, but I don't know who else may have the information he was holding over my head.

I couldn't care less if the information sinks my adoptive father's political career or not. But I do care about the bill we've worked so hard on for the past two years, one that could improve the lives of foster children around the country. Just a few more months, and once it passes, I'll truly be free to move on with my life. Maybe that step will include renewing my friendship with Liam and Diana.

I bite down on the insides of my cheeks to keep myself from smiling. I can't smile at my husband's funeral. But God, it's going to be so good to talk to them, even if it's just for a few hurried seconds. For the first time in nearly a year, it doesn't feel like the world is ending.

"...congratulations on your engagement."

It takes a moment for the words to penetrate the rise and fall of conversation around me. I swallow hard, try to fight the sudden fluttering panic inside my chest.

It can't be. It's not possible.

I turn to look, just in time to see Liam slipping an arm around Diana's waist and pulling her against him.

My heart shatters. For one moment, I feel it all. Heartbreak, grief, fury, jealousy.

Why her? Why not me?

Knowing he would never settle down had made watching the parade of women streaming in and out of his life tolerable. But this…this is more painful than anything I've ever experienced. All these years I told myself Liam would never settle down, would never see me as more than a friend. It made it easier when his picture appeared in the paper or online with yet another woman on his arm at some gala or fundraiser. Made forcing myself to date and picture a life with someone else bearable.

And now he's engaged to one of my best friends. How can I renew our friendship now? How can I pretend like I'm happy for them, stand up at their wedding, hold their children…

My stomach pitches up. I can't. I can never be friends with them again.

I've lost everything.

Then, as if my will has asserted itself over my heart, everything vanishes. The shock, the anger, the heartache. All that's left is a yawning emptiness. I slip into that blank space, embrace the nothingness.

"Aislinn?"

I blink. Stephanie is in front of me. The couple I was talking to have moved off to the side but are looking at me with concern, as are several people in line. Including Diana and Li—

No.

Stephanie reaches out and grabs my hand. I start to pull away but force myself to stop. Hurt flares in her eyes, but I ignore it. "Are you all right?"

I nod and gently pat the back of her hand. "Yes. Just tired." I force a tiny smile for the benefit of anyone watching before I withdraw my fingers from her grasp. "As well as I can be."

"You can take a break."

"No." I swallow, tamp down my anger. "I just want to get through this."

I angle myself away before she can push me anymore. Angle toward Liam and Diana as I steel myself against the storm of emotions seething inside my chest.

Diana's tentative smile nearly breaks me as she clutches her hands in front of her. The ring glitters, taunts. "Hi, Aislinn."

Strong. I have to stay strong. I've been stronger than I ever realized I could be these past few months.

Just a little longer, I promise myself. *Then you can rest.* "Hello, Diana."

Her face falls. She glances at Liam, but he doesn't look at her. Instead, he's staring at me, suspicion evident in his ice-blue eyes. It makes it easier to steady myself. To put him in the role of villain instead of the just-out-of-reach hero he's played for so long in my dreams.

"We're sorry for your loss," he murmurs, his voice cool and formal.

"Thank you." I force out my next words. "Congratulations on your engagement."

Diana blinks, a tiny furrow appearing between her dark brows. "You... Did you not know?"

I thread my fingers together. Focus on the pain of squeezing my hands together so hard my knuckles turn white. "No."

Diana glances up at Liam, but he continues to stare at me, his gaze probing. Assessing.

I stand my ground and stare right back. Yes, I've lied, covered for a man who sold his vote for a ticket to a senator's office. But Liam lied, too. He lied to me since the first week I met him when he told me he would never get married.

Pain and anger push at the edges of my control. I push back. I need the emptiness. Need to not only get through this but erase any feelings I ever carried for Liam Whitlock.

Diana clears her throat. "Maybe we could all get together in a few weeks."

Her invitation, coupled with her shy smile and the glimmer of hope in her eyes, makes me tremble. Waver. She's innocent in all of this.

Then her hand comes up to brush a stray lock of hair out of her face. The ring glimmers in the light. Maybe once I would have been capable of putting Diana and whatever happiness she's found with Liam above my own heartbreak.

But the woman I've had to become isn't.

"Perhaps." I nod to the line behind them. "I wish I could talk longer now, but—"

"Of course." I swallow back a bitter taste in my throat as Diana grabs Liam's hand and tugs him forward. "Just… we're here, Aislinn. Always."

I nod, not trusting myself to speak. I meet Liam's gaze one final time. Emotions surge. Loathing tangles with love. I stare at his face, the familiar dark lashes framing ice-blue eyes, the faintest hint of the dimple in one cheek, the strong point of his chin. Remember the countless movie nights, dinners and festivals we attended, the midnight conversations as we shared our dreams for our futures.

And then I turn my back. They're no longer a part of my future.

CHAPTER TWO

Liam

Four months later

A TUXEDOED WAITER passes by with a tray of glass flutes filled with sparkling champagne. A jazz band, set up at the far end of the ballroom, is playing an energetic song. A surprising number of people are on the dance floor. The mood is happy, excited, joyful.

Normally, I would try to match their energy, plaster a smile on my face and pretend. But I don't want to. Not tonight. Not after a year of digging and investigating and coming up against wall after wall. Not after investing my fortune in building up my own company, only to have one of my most important prospective clients inform me that my supposed broken engagement a few months prior had damaged my reputation to the point where he was considering no longer working with me. And he wasn't the only one.

I breathe in deeply in an effort to combat the tension tightening my shoulders. I have done so much for Aislinn, even if she doesn't know it. And now I'm prepared to do even more.

I glance around the ballroom, frowning when I don't see her face. I've attended so many events like this over the years, many of them planned by Aislinn for her adoptive father's various campaign events, fundraisers and galas. She's usually front and center, greeting people like long-lost friends and ensuring glasses and plates are full.

My lips twitch. It's been twelve years since I sat in our high school theater, sullen and irritated that my counselor, Mrs. Scout, had dragged me out of study hall to meet two other foster kids she thought I'd "connect" with. Diana hadn't had the same chip on her shoulder, but she'd carried the same reserve.

And then Aislinn had bounced down the aisle, golden hair tied up in a ponytail and a huge smile on her face. I'd watched Diana visibly thaw in front of me as the sophomore with the shining green eyes and eager voice had told her how beautiful her hair was, how she wished she had Diana's height, how she was so excited to get to know her.

Then she'd looked at me. Her eyes had widened slightly. And then she'd smiled shyly and told me she was excited to get to know me, too.

The friendship that was established that day in the dim theater with the threadbare seats and a cast singing "Without Love" off-key on the stage was the first time in eight years I'd let anyone get close. Diana and I bonded over our shared trauma of being thrust from our former lives into foster care. And Aislinn…

I smile slightly. Aislinn may be the youngest of our trio, but she's always been the mother of the group. She never wanted anyone to feel left out. She saw the best in everyone, even when I didn't.

My hands curl into a fist at my side. Is that what happened with her husband? Did she meet him at an event like this, or did he reach out, make her feel special, and prey on her naive nature before he pulled her into his world?

"Liam?"

My head snaps around. Eric is standing a few feet away, his brow furrowed.

"Are you all right?"

I force my lips into some semblance of a smile and nod. "Congratulations, Senator."

Eric's smile is equally tight, strained. "Thank you."

"Where's Aislinn?"

I don't bother with niceties. I've wasted over a year trying to be methodical, thorough. Trying to do things the right way and not stir the pot. I'm done playing nice.

Eric's eyes flicker up to the series of balconies ringing the upper gallery of the ballroom. "Somewhere up there."

"An odd place for her to be."

Eric's smile disappears. "Everything's been off. Ever since…" He catches himself, clears his throat. "Maybe you can get through to her."

"Doubt it," I grumble under my breath as Eric walks away to greet someone.

It's been radio silence ever since the funeral. Diana, I know, has continued to text her weekly. She recently added an invitation to her upcoming engagement party to my brother.

I wince as I stride across the ballroom toward a marble staircase that circles up to the second floor. It's still odd to think of Diana and my half brother, Ari, being engaged. Getting married. Being in love. Considering I didn't even know I had a half brother until this past spring, finding out that he and Diana had had a one-night stand had been jarring. Not as jarring, though, as realizing they genuinely loved each other. A situation made all the more awkward by Diana's and my fake engagement.

I take the steps two at a time. I had met Dexter a total of three times before he did us all a favor and died. The first had been after Aislinn had stopped hanging out with Diana and me. It wasn't just being busy at work; she'd stopped responding to our group texts and had sent several of my calls to voicemail. So, I'd gone over to her apartment to check on her.

It was seven in the morning. Dexter had opened the door. I'd hated him on sight. Silver hair mussed. Rumpled dress shirt. Belt undone. Even though he was over twenty years older than me, plenty of women would have found him attractive. But when he shot me that slow, smug smile, I barely resisted punching him in the face. He informed me Aislinn was in the shower and would contact me later.

She never did. But I started seeing plenty of photos of them plastered on social media and the occasional feature in the *New York Times* about their attendance at some fancy dinner or political event.

I reach the top of the stairs and glance over the railing. Eric is still chatting with someone. My eyes roam over the ballroom until I see Stephanie, Aislinn's adoptive mother, standing off to the side.

Eric and Aislinn had always had a warm friendship, but as Aislinn had told us, there had always been a distance between them, a recognition that she was not Eric's biological daughter. She'd sworn up and down that everything Eric had provided her with was enough. I knew she was lying, but pressing her on it would have only made her sad. And she had Stephanie, the woman she called Mom and who returned Aislinn's love tenfold.

But from what little Stephanie had said when I'd finally gone to her after months of no contact, Aislinn had cooled things between them, too. Yes, she and Dexter had accompanied Eric and Stephanie to plenty of events around town during their whirlwind courtship and brief marriage. But it was like Aislinn's soul had disappeared, replaced by someone cold, empty.

I start to walk the gallery. How Aislinn had survived her entire life in foster care and still managed to come out with stars in her eyes was a miracle I had no desire to taint. I worried about her sometimes, especially when she started dating in college. Worried no man would ever be able to be enough for someone so…good.

Never in a million years would I have pictured her marrying a government contractor nearly twice her age with a reputation for cruelty in his business dealings.

A man who only escaped being charged with fraud and financial crimes by dying of an unexpected heart attack.

I walk along the gallery, passing behind thick pillars and the occasional alcove shrouded in darkness. All but one. The last alcove before the gallery gives way to three stories of glass overlooking the Hudson River. The doorway is framed by deep red velvet curtains held back with gold ties.

I stop in the doorway, hands in my pockets, shoulders thrown back. Ready to do battle. Instead, I freeze.

I know the woman in front of me. I know the delicate shape of her face, the full lips I'm used to seeing curved in a smile, the big green eyes that could see good in the absolute worst moments. Eyes that calmed me when I was at my worst, held the simmering anger I've never fully been able to escape from since I was placed in foster care.

But now, the green eyes staring at me are anything but

warm and soothing. They're ice-cold, void of emotion. Her lips are painted red, a shade that complements her sleekly styled golden hair. It's shorter now, styled to accentuate her sculpted cheekbones and the stubborn point of her chin. She's dressed in black, lounging on a white divan with one slender arm draped across the back and her other hand cradling a glass of amber liquid. She doesn't break eye contact as she raises the glass to her lips.

Heat jolts through me as her lips close around the rim. *What the hell?*

I mentally take a step back. This is Aislinn. A woman I've known since she was sixteen years old. A little sister, someone to be protected and cared for, not lusted after.

"You're wearing black."

She tilts the glass back, takes a long sip. The heat starts to rise again, but I squelch it. It's been nearly a year since I've dated. My reaction is strictly biology. And, I think grimly, if Aislinn accepts my proposal, it's going to be even longer before I indulge in sex again. But the return on that investment will far outweigh the costs. Returns that will benefit both Aislinn and me, given our current predicaments.

"Haven't you heard? I'm in mourning."

Her voice is deeper. There's no light, no whisper of joy beneath everyday words. I'm staring at a wraith, a shadow of who Aislinn used to be.

Cold fingers wrap around my heart. Squeeze. All these months I told myself something else was going on. Told Diana over and over whenever she started to doubt. Yet as I watch Aislinn's calm, blank stare, I can't help but wonder if I'm wrong.

"I heard about the Department of Justice."

She blinks. Diana and I always used to tease her about

her inability to play poker or any other sort of game where she had to conceal her emotions. She's always been an open book. But now, I can't get a read on her. Can't reach her even though she's just a few feet away.

She stands in one smooth movement, the soft silk folds of her dress following the curve of her hips, the length of her. My eyes flick back up.

"You and the rest of New York." One corner of her mouth tilts up. "Really, the world at this point."

She swishes past me. A dark scent teases me, rose with a hint of spice. The exact opposite of the light, floral scent she always used to wear. Some daisy perfume that came in a bottle shaped like the flower.

I turn, my entire body tensing at the sight of her bare back. Aside from the ties at her shoulders, there's nothing. Nothing but smooth, pale skin all the way down to the base of her spine. Thankfully, silk covers her backside. But with the way it clings, it doesn't leave anything to the imagination. If I didn't think it would piss her off, I'd offer her my coat.

She moves on to the gallery, stopping with one hand on the banister as she gazes down at the ballroom. I follow, stopping just a few feet behind her.

"What are you going to do?"

She turns her head just enough so that her face is in profile. The gentle slope and slight upturn of her nose, the elegant definition of her jaw, the long line of her neck backlit by the golden glow from the ballroom. "Not much I can do."

Anger surges through me. How can she be so blasé about this? "Do you even comprehend the enormity of their decision? The impact it will have on your finances?"

She turns away, giving me the back of her head. Another dismissal. One that has me gritting my teeth.

Has she forgotten everything we've been through? How our friendship was forged in literally saving a life? The years of supporting each other as we fought our way out of high school, through college and to careers and adulthood? She doesn't know the lengths Diana and I went to protect her, doesn't know the engagement was fake. But damn it, we gave up everything to keep her safe. And for what? For her to act like this is all a game?

"It's not just the Department of Justice." I should stop talking, but her silence grates on my last nerve. "The FBI and IRS are both involved, too. All of Dexter's properties were bought with money tied to his criminal activities. You don't have a place to live, and last I heard, most of your finances were tied to his, so you have no money."

"I'm aware."

The anger twists, morphs into fury. I close the distance between us, place my hand on one bare shoulder and turn her to face me. Her skin heats the palm of my hand, feeds my anger. And, deep beneath that, fear. She's right in front of me for the first time in months, and she's never been further away.

"So you're going to do nothing? Just treat this like you have the last year of your life?"

She raises her chin. Then, with defiance flashing in her eyes, she tilts her glass up and throws back the rest. Whiskey, I realize as I smell caramel and vanilla tangled with oak.

"I didn't say that." She sets her empty glass away from her on the banister, then faces the ballroom again. "I submitted my notice to Eric this afternoon."

Eric. Not Dad. Even though they had never been as close as she and Stephanie, she had always called him Dad.

"Why? You love your job."

"And my personal link to a corrupt man could harm his reelection campaign next year."

My head snaps around, my eyes cutting to Eric. He's standing next to Stephanie now, their heads bowed together. They suddenly don't look like the elegant older couple I've always known, but tired, haggard.

"He said that?"

"In less explicit terms, yes."

I think I hear the slightest hitch in Aislinn's voice. But when I glance through the corner of my eye, her face is still set in that blank mask.

"I solved the problem by turning in my resignation, effective after tonight."

I grasp the banister with both hands, curl my fingers around it. "Damn it, Aislinn, you're good at what you do. Everyone knows you were the soul behind the Foster Care Protection Act. You can't let a few rumors drive you out." I want to grab her by the shoulders and shake her. "You can't just give up."

I feel more than see the intention that grips her. I sense the emotion that flashes through her instead of seeing it. But I know it's there. Thank God.

"I call it surviving."

"Semantics," I snap back.

She swallows hard. Her chin dips as she inhales. "Call it what you want, Liam." She spits out my name like its poison. "It's always easier to judge from the outside looking in."

I mentally take a step back. Yes, I'm furious. Hurt. Diana and I have been worried sick about her for months, yet she's rejected us at every turn, making bad choice after bad choice as she spiraled down so fast we couldn't reach out and grab her. Save her.

But I can save her now. I can save us both.

"You don't want to leave." I keep my tone gentle, my voice quiet and as close to friendly as I can manage. I'll never get her to confide in me, to consider my plan, if I'm constantly putting her on the defensive.

I wait. Below us, the music transitions from lively and joyful to something slower, a deep, sultry tune that makes the air feel thicker.

Then, at last, a sigh, so quiet it's almost inaudible below the music. "I don't know what I want."

When I look at her this time, the grief in her eyes is one I feel all the way to my bones. It's always been like this, ever since I first laid eyes on her in our high school theater. She wore her emotions so openly, shared them willingly with no strings attached. I hate seeing her like this, feeling the sadness I'm convinced she's kept from me, kept from Diana, for nearly a year. But a sick, selfish part of me is just so fucking glad she's finally letting me in.

I follow her gaze down to Eric and Stephanie. This time, my anger is directed at the man I'm now convinced has a role in whatever mess she's been caught up in. "He never should have accepted your resignation."

"It was the right choice for his campaign." Her sigh is sad, heavy. "The financial investigation may have cleared me of wrongdoing, but that doesn't mean the public believes it. There are several high-ranking donors who have voiced their displeasure. Eric had to make a choice."

"You're his daughter."

Her shoulders fall a fraction. "But I'm not."

This time, when I lay my hand on her shoulder, I do so gently. My fingers press down on her bare skin. I remove my hand before I let my fingertips trail down her arm. A gesture I've done a thousand times since knowing her. Except right now, it doesn't feel right. Too intimate. "You don't have to face this alone."

She's still quiet, but I can see the cracks in the mask. Can see glimmers of the woman I knew beneath. My friend.

"I have a plan."

A shutter drops down over her face. She takes a step back. "Of course you have a plan." Her voice is cold once more. "You always have a plan."

Insulted, I glare down at her. "You used to like my plans."

She looks back out over the ballroom. "I'm listening."

"As long as your finances are tied up, you don't have much in the way of resources. Especially if you're not working. You need money. Support."

"I need money." Her head swings back around, her blue eyes cool. "I don't need support. I can take care of myself."

The words throw me. I miss Aislinn, miss who she used to be. But I also remember the times she would get caught up in separating emotion from fact, when she would fail to stand up for herself because she didn't want to hurt someone else's feelings. I hate the reason for it, but I can't help but admire the backbone she's displaying in the midst of her life literally falling apart.

"Okay. No support. But you need money. Something to keep you afloat while this investigation drags out. And given that Eric accepted your resignation, I'm guessing you're not going to be getting much from him."

A low blow, but it lands. Her lips thin as her eyes narrow. "I'm not asking him for a damn thing."

"Well, then you need money. And I need a wife."

CHAPTER THREE

Aislinn

MY TRAITOROUS HEART LEAPS. I indulge it for one moment, allowing myself to pretend that Liam actually wants me to be his wife because he's finally realized, after all these years, that he's in love with me just as deeply and irrevocably as I have been with him since I first laid eyes on him.

And then, with the mental snap of my fingers, I suffer the hope and force myself back into reality.

Liam stands in front of me, looking ridiculously handsome in a black suit and tie. There's a smugness about his lips, a confidence in the arrogant tilt of his chin. I hate how handsome he is. I hate how much he still affects me, how I knew he was approaching even before he appeared in the doorway of the alcove.

I once thought my love for him was romantic, an unrequited love story that would match the great romances of literature. I'm a damn fool. There was nothing romantic about how I felt about him. Pathetic, naive, ridiculous—those are far more accurate. Even now, I know he's not proposing marriage because he's had an epiphany. Like he said, he has a plan. He always has a plan. One that takes him one step closer to his ultimate goal of achieving success. A success that does not include goals like mine: a family. Children. Liam's goals include financial success, vacation homes in the Caribbean, maybe even one day a private jet.

I focus on those facts, on how wrong we are for each other, as I gather my next words. "I don't see the correlation between my needing money and you needing a wife."

It's petty, but I enjoy the flash of irritation on his handsome face.

"I'm proposing we marry, Aislinn," he says.

I hold his gaze as long as I can before I look back down at the ballroom. It takes every ounce of effort to conceal my heartbreak. There have been so many times over the past year that I thought I'd been at my breaking point, thought I couldn't possibly sink any lower than I already have. And yet, every single time, I've been wrong. And, I remind myself every single time, I've risen above it. Survived.

"What about Diana?" I ask.

"As I'm sure you're aware, she's engaged to my brother."

Ah. Second best. I hate that I'm envious of Diana. Jealous of her and whatever she and Liam shared. In that moment, I hate Liam for placing me between the two of them.

"Why do you need a wife?" I demand. "You said you'd never get married."

"I'm starting my own firm."

"I remember."

"The clients I've been working with lately are traditionalists. They see marriage as a sign of stability."

I think back to the rotating cast of faces Liam has

dated over the years. "Not the word I would use to describe your love life."

He arches one brow. "I didn't realize you paid attention."

Oh, more than you know.

"There were concerns raised about my age, experience and reputation. And when Diana's engagement ended, it caused even more problems."

I frown. "Is that why you got engaged in the first place?"

The singer's voice fills the silence between us, deep and sultry. I force myself to look at him even as I see the answer in Liam's eyes before he says it out loud.

"No. We—"

"Stop." I step back, look back down at the couples swaying in each other's arms to the seductive music. "That's between you and Diana."

"Aislinn—"

"No, Liam." My voice whips out, rough and furious. "I don't want to hear it."

I can't hear that he cared for Diana the way I always wanted him to care for me. Can't hear that Diana will always be the one that got away.

His shoulders shift back as his eyes narrow. I know he's getting ready to argue with me, so I rush on.

"So now you're proposing to me."

He pauses. Watches me. Then he replies with a simple, "Yes." Factual. To the point. No flowery words, no attempts to pretend like this is anything but what it is: a business arrangement.

"I hardly think the widow of a government contractor whose entire estate has been seized by the government and who, until just recently, was under investigation for any links to her husband's crimes is the kind of candidate your clients would accept."

A slow, smug smile crosses his face. "Except you've been officially cleared. And two of my clients hated your husband. When it was announced that you were under investigation, both of them thought you were innocent."

I tap my fingers on the banister. "You've been talking about me with your clients?"

"They brought it up. It's a huge case, Aislinn. Of course people are talking about it."

"So, what? Because they hated Dexter, they'll just accept you marrying me less than a year after my husband died? That doesn't sound like the kind of 'traditional' union they expect out of you."

"They will accept the aggrieved widow of a man many suspect pressured you into marriage. There's also the romance of the situation."

Oh God. This whole situation is so fantastically horrible I don't know whether to laugh or cry. "Romance?"

"Childhood friends. Years of loving friendship. You got married, so I got engaged to Diana. Wrong choice and one made out of heartbreak instead of love. A fact Diana and I both realized and ended the engagement."

Wow. Perfectly spun lies about why people would actually believe we were together, spoken so genuinely I could see people falling for it.

Disgust slithers through me. Did I ever really know him? Or did I blind myself to who he truly was? *Just like Eric.* My stomach rolls. I once thought I was a good judge of character. Another lie I told myself. "Sounds like I'm the perfect candidate for what you have in mind."

"You are."

Not because he loves me. Not because he's had an

epiphany and realized he can't live without me. I'm the perfect candidate because I can elicit sympathy, tug on heartstrings with my pathetic fall from grace while making Liam look like someone he's not.

"No."

Liam blinks. "No?"

"No." I incline my head. "You have a lengthy list of past girlfriends and lovers. One of them can fill the role."

"I don't want anyone else."

Heat pricks my eyes. I have to leave. I start to move past him, but he shifts.

"Aislinn."

His voice whispers across my skin, sinks down into my veins. The sound of my name on his lips, spoken with such concern and affection, is pure temptation. One I desperately want to surrender to.

"I can help you, too."

I stare down at the floor. "How?"

"Marry me. You'll have a home, clothes—"

My head snaps up. Fury barrels through me. "So I'm going to be what? A pet?"

I spent months under Dexter's thumb. Now I'm living by the whims of federal government. I may have lost everything—my career, financial security, my friends—but I'll be damned if I give up my freedom again.

"No." He sounds genuinely shocked, frustrated. "It would just be to help you—"

"I don't want your help. Goodbye, Liam."

I brush past him and walk down the gallery. The music transitions from the slow, burning love song to another up-beat tune. I hurry down the stairs, not bothering to see if Liam is behind me or not. I have to put as much distance between us. Have to get out of this hell and back to…

My steps slow as I near the bottom. I pause, lean against the cool marble wall for a moment. I have nowhere to go. I gave up my apartment when I married Dexter. The FBI seized his house in Greenwich and the Park Avenue penthouse. Stephanie offered up the guesthouse at her and Eric's estate in Bedford. But I can't be around them. Not after Eric accepted my resignation without so much as a word of resistance.

A tiny part of me wants to accept what Liam is offering. I wouldn't have his love, but I'd have him in my life again. A touch of normalcy, a chance to rest.

Tempting. But I'm done being a convenience for the men in my life, being of use until they decide they no longer need me.

No more.

I square my shoulders and walk down the remaining stairs. I'll get a hotel room for a couple nights, find a short-term rental. I'll find a job by the end of the week. I worked for a cleaning service in college and even bartended one summer to pay for a trip with Liam and Diana to Paris. Not where I saw my career in my late twenties. But I have skills. I can take care of myself. I don't want to leave New York, but if that's what it will take for me to survive, so be it.

I skirt around the edges of the ballroom and slip into the hotel lobby. Guests mill around, but thankfully no one looks twice at me. Most days I can handle the curious glances, the accusing stares when I walk through the building Eric's New York office is housed in.

Right now, though, I just want to go to a hotel—one I can afford—and fall asleep.

"Mrs. Simpson."

My shoulders climb up before I can stop them. I hate

the sound of my married name. I haven't heard it in months, didn't think I would hear it again. So when I turn to face the man who uttered it with such casual familiarity, I'm angry.

Angry and instantly on guard as soon as I lay eyes on him. Tall, nearly as tall as Liam, but broader with thick shoulders, beefy arms and a slight smile that leaves a chill in its wake.

"I go by Miss Knightley now."

He doesn't shift. Doesn't blink. Just continues to stare with that tiny, creepy smile. "I'm sorry about your husband."

Few people at the funeral seemed genuinely remorseful about Dexter's passing. But beneath the blankness, there's a glimmer of glee. As if he's enjoying this.

The chill digs into my skin. "Thank you."

"Perhaps he mentioned me. Augustus Marston."

"No. He didn't. If you'll excuse me—"

Marston's hand shoots out and clamps down on my wrist. His palm is dry, cold, his grasp too tight.

Panic flutters in my chest. I force myself to stay still. He strikes me as the kind of man who wants me to be afraid, to run so he can chase. I raise my chin. Liam accused me of running away. He doesn't know how capable I am of fighting. No one does. "Are you planning on engaging in kidnapping tonight, Mr. Marston?"

His slow, reptilian blink is a victory. "No. Of course not, Mrs. Simpson." His leer deepens. "Excuse me. Miss Knightley. This is a business meeting."

I glance down at his hand. "Feels more like the beginning of unlawful restraint."

Augustus slowly releases me. "Dexter said you were timid."

"Dexter was a bastard."

Marston's chuckle sounds like the beginnings of a cartoon villain laugh. "Agreed. Which is why I'm here. Dexter owed me fifty thousand dollars. I'm here to collect."

Now it's my turn to blink. "Excuse me?"

"Fifty thousand. A high-stakes poker game he lost two days before he died." The smile vanishes. "I want my money."

"As I'm sure you're aware, I have no money." My voice stays level even as the fear deepens. I can handle dealing with the FBI and any other federal agency. But a poker boss I'm guessing has very strong ties to the criminal underworld in New York is something else entirely.

"You're too modest." He leans down. "Your adoptive father is worth an estimated four million dollars. You've rubbed plenty of…shoulders in your line of work. Politicians, investors, bankers, movie stars. You have multiple resources."

"And that's where you and I differ," I snap back. "I don't ask other people for money."

His eyes harden. "Then we have a problem."

Dreams of a quiet night disappear. The flickering hope that maybe, just maybe, the worst is now truly behind me evaporates. I'm in the lobby of one of the most glamorous hotels in New York surrounded by people. And I've never been more alone.

"I'm not involving anyone else in this." I maintain his gaze even though I want to sink into the floor. Want to throw back my head and scream. "What about a payment plan—"

"As you just pointed out, you have no money. As of tonight, according to my sources, no steady source of income." The smile returns, sharp and predatory. "Payment

in full in one week or we'll have to work out another...
arrangement."

The suggestion in his voice makes me want to gag. I
managed to keep Dexter off me throughout the duration
of our relationship. I'm not going to give my body to another man against my will.

But Marston won't play fair. There won't be any investigation, no due process or day in court. There will just be
yet another man pressuring me, hunting me.

Bone-deep exhaustion seeps in. I'm suddenly so tired I
can barely stand. I suck in a quick breath as the fear starts
to take over. When will this end? I just need this to end.

No. I'm not going to let this be the moment that breaks
me. I've come too far, survived too much, to let this man
I've never met take control of my story now.

I lean in, close the distance between us. Marston moves
back, just a fraction but enough to give me a desperately
needed sense of power.

"I would rather jump in the Hudson in the middle of
winter than spend another second in your company, let
alone your bed," I spit out. "Unlike Dexter, I keep my
promises. So you can either get your money in time, or I
will use every single one of my connections to drag you
into the spotlight and ruin you."

Marston reaches up, runs a finger down my hair. "I
like your spirit, Miss Knightley."

I barely hold in my shudder. I'm about to retort when
awareness pricks the back of my neck. My spine straight-
ens a second before Marston's gaze shifts to a point over
my shoulder. My satisfaction at seeing the blood leach out
of his face is short-lived as Liam speaks from behind me.

"Hello, Marston."

CHAPTER FOUR

Aislinn

I WHIRL AROUND. Liam is standing just a couple feet behind me. The rage etched onto his handsome face catapults me back to another cold winter's day, one where I barely stopped Liam from killing Diana's foster father. His neck is corded, his pulse throbbing in his temple. Marston's eyes were blank, like staring into a void. But Liam's pale blue eyes are sharpened into icy daggers.

My gaze drops down. Liam's hands are curled into fists.

"Liam." I keep my voice gentle, my tone soft as I approach him slowly. "Liam, I'm all right."

Slowly, he drags his attention away from Marston and looks down at me. He grabs my wrist and starts to tug me to his side, his fingers gentle on the skin Marston gripped so hard just a couple ago. I wince.

Liam's gaze shifts down. I follow his eyes, see the lingering red marks from Marston's grip. "You're not all right." The guttural growl of his voice shocks me. Before I can reply, he steps forward and inserts himself between

Marston and me. "I didn't think you were this stupid, Marston."

I tilt my head so I can see around Liam. If I thought Marston pale before, it's nothing compared to the whites of his eyes blending into the chalkiness of his skin. His lips stretch into another smile. But this one is forced and full of fear as he inclines his head to Liam.

"Mr. Whitlock." He clears his throat. "I didn't realize you and Miss Knightley were acquainted."

"Engaged."

My mouth drops open. "Liam—"

"Do you have a problem with my fiancée?"

Marston withers before my eyes. His shoulders curl in as he glances at me, then quickly looks down. "I didn't realize…when?"

"A recent development." Liam's voice is razor-sharp and furious. "Answer my question. Is there a problem?"

Marston slowly inclines his head in a deferential gesture I'd enjoy if Liam wasn't inserting himself into my problems. "A misunderstanding. That's all."

"Good. I'd hate to have to reach out to my lawyers or the FBI."

"No need." Marston clears his throat again. "Consider the debt paid in full." He nods to me. "My apologies for any inconvenience, Miss Knightley."

He's gone before I can say anything. I stand there, questions whirling through my mind. Why is a poker boss scared of Liam? How does Liam know him? Did Marston truly forgive the debt, or was this just to satisfy Liam and he'll come after me later?

And why did Liam call me his…

"Fiancée?" I choke out the word as Liam turns around to face me.

"It worked. He made an assumption. I played along."

My fingers curl around my clutch. Better than slapping him across the face in a lobby crowded with people. "If you have that kind of power over him, you could have just told him to leave me alone."

"Claiming you as mine will ensure your safety."

Mine. The word pulses between us. His eyes flare for a split second, ice to fire in the span of a heartbeat. But it's gone so quickly I wonder if I've imagined it.

Wished it, I think grimly. Even now, after everything, there's still a stupid part of me clinging to broken dreams. "And ensure you get what you wanted."

I nearly flinch as his gaze turns glacial. "Your opinion of me has certainly dropped."

I start to speak, but the all-too familiar sound of a camera clicking has me turning my head. There's a photographer ten feet away, a young woman dressed in black pants and a glittering black top. She snaps another photo before turning and darting toward the door.

"Security!" Liam bellows. "Stop her!"

The guard near the door lunges but just barely misses grabbing the photographer as she rushes out onto the street. Faces swivel from the door back to Liam and me as the room quiets for one second. Then the noise rises once more. Voices chattering, swirling around me as I stand in the midst of a vortex of public speculation.

"Was that a pickpocket?"

"Did you see what happened?"

"Wait, isn't that the senator's adopted kid? The one who married that man who…"

My heartbeat surges as invisible fingers dig into my chest and squeeze. My breathing quickens. A hot flush smothers my skin like a heavy blanket I can't escape from.

The fear pushes to the surface, orders me to find an exit. Escape.

"Liam." I manage to gasp out his name even as my throat tightens. Before I can look up to see if he's heard me, a strong arm wraps around my waist. I lean into the comforting heat of his body.

"Aislinn?"

"I…" Heat pricks my eyes. "Help me. Please."

I've barely finished speaking when Liam dips and scoops me into his arms. I cling to him, not caring how I look, what people think. I just need him to get me out of here.

Liam's arms tighten around me. "Almost there."

The cold winter air is harsh against my bare back as he walks outside. More flashes go off, light after light, voices shouting. My heartbeat accelerates, pounds against my ribs so hard I'm sure it's going to burst out of my chest. I try to fight it, to remember the grounding techniques the counselor taught me. But there's so much noise, and I just need it to stop, or I won't be able to breathe—

"I've got you, Aislinn."

His voice penetrates. I mentally latch onto the sound of his voice, sink into it. I bury my face into his neck and breathe in the warm spiciness of his cologne. A scent he's been wearing for years. I release a shuddering breath as the familiarity of it washes over me, takes the edge off my panic.

"Hold on."

A moment later he eases me into the back of a vehicle. The door closes, shutting out the lights and the noise. It comes back for a split second when another door opens. I hear more shouts, but try to shut them out as I focus on the sounds around me. The quiet murmur of the radio. The loud click of the other door closing, followed by the softer click of a seat belt. I wiggle my fingertips, then clench and unclench my hands. Each sound, each movement, gradually lessens the tightness in my chest. My heart is still racing, my breathing still fast. But the panic is receding.

I force my eyes open. Buttery leather seats on the opposite side of what I now realize is a limo. The lights of New York outside my window.

And Liam sitting next to me.

Slowly, bit by bit, I regain control. My breathing slows, as does my pulse. The pain in my chest eases. But it leaves room for the subsequent exhaustion to rush in, drag my eyelids down as I sink into the seat. I'm too tired to be embarrassed by letting Liam see what I've been struggling with for months.

"How long?"

My head lolls back against the headrest. "What?"

"The panic attacks."

I want to reply with something smart. But it would take too much effort, so I opt for the simple truth. "Eight months."

Dexter and I had argued. I'd started for the door. He'd grabbed my arm, swung me around and flung me onto the couch. When I'd tried to get up, he'd pushed me back down into the cushions, held me there as my pulse had skyrocketed and my breathing had started coming out in sharp, frantic gasps. When it was finally over, and I'd become aware of my surroundings again, Dexter had been sitting in the chair across from me, a brandy in one hand and a sneer of disgust on his face.

"So fucking weak."

The words had been a switch. One minute I'd felt disoriented, violated, frail. The next I'd been…empty.

Felt nothing. A merciful nothing that had kept me sane through the tangled mess of my new life.

But I can't tell Liam any of that. Don't want him to hear how feeble I'd been. I breathe in a deep, cleansing breath. "I'm seeing a therapist."

"That's a start."

"Don't." I slightly shake my head. "This isn't your fight, Liam." God, I can't even open my eyes. I've always experienced exhaustion after the attacks, but never this acute.

"It is now."

"We are *not* engaged." I force myself to open my eyes, to meet his gaze. "Marston is the only one who heard you. Given that he's a poker boss at best and probably has ties to organized crime, I doubt the press are going to pay attention to him."

Liam stares at me for a long moment. Then he shrugs. *Shrugs.* Like the fake engagement or marriage or whatever scheme Liam concocted isn't that big of a deal. Except to him, it's probably not. The marriage isn't important. The boost to his image is.

"Where should I take you?" he asks quietly.

I hesitate. "Chelsea."

"You moved?"

"Temporary lodgings."

"Address."

I wince. "Could you make that sound less like a bark and more like a request?"

"No."

I mentally roll my eyes. "It's a hotel, Liam."

"A hotel."

Fatigue pulls at me, whispers in my ear and encourages me to just tune Liam out for a moment. "Yes. Until I can make other arrangements."

"Why didn't you reach out to Diana and me?"

Pain tightens my chest. *Because I couldn't. Because I was trying to keep you safe.* "Things change, Liam." I can't fight it anymore. I relax back into the leather. "I appreciate your help tonight. Would you wake me up when we get there?"

I hear a muted reply but can't discern the words. I try to process, then quickly give up as I spiral down into a blissful state of nothing.

Liam

The limo stops outside the brownstone home in the quieter Upper East Side. It's been twenty minutes, and already security at Fifty-seventh Street notified me there are paparazzi on the sidewalk outside my penthouse in Billionaires' Row. It's only a couple miles away, but we might as well be in an entirely different world inside this peaceful, elm-lined corridor.

Aislinn wanted to believe no one heard our run-in with Marston, so I dropped it, let her have a few minutes to rest. But my instinct was right. There's no way out but forward.

My eyes flick to Aislinn, still asleep on the opposite side of the car. She'd been so focused on Marston and then me, she'd failed to notice how many people have been paying attention to our little drama unfolding.

I rub at my jaw. I'd been so focused on her that I had failed to notice the photographers by the door until they'd raised their cameras.

My phone dings again. I glance down and stifle a groan when I see Diana's name on the screen. It's the third time she's called in seven minutes. I send this one to voice-mail, too.

I'm not worried about her being angry or jealous. Our engagement was fake. There wasn't a single moment during our whole charade when I experienced anything but the same feelings of friendship we'd had for years. On the few occasions I've seen Diana and my brother together, the way she looks at him and he at her, almost made me envious for a relationship like theirs.

Almost. I wish them well. I want nothing but happiness for them. But I also know how cruel life can be, how swiftly it changes from light to dark. I have no desire to invite the potential for loss back into my life. It's one of the reasons I've struggled to bond with Ari.

I glance over at Aislinn again. Strands of gold have fallen across her face. Her lips are parted, her breathing even and peaceful. Her face is relaxed, serene, yet I can still see the darkness etched into her skin beneath her eyes. The responses I've had tonight—the awareness, the small flares of attraction—are concerning. Not once did I experience this with Diana, and that was after touching her, dancing with her, pretending to be in love.

My phone chimes, signaling a text message. I open it and grimace when I see Diana's screenshot of me carrying Aislinn out of the hotel, her head tucked into the crook of my neck. A social media post with the caption Crook's widow already engaged to legendary investor!

I'll get my feelings under control. There is no other choice. The news is out, and we have to move forward. Starting with finding a safe place for Aislinn to stay.

Anger stirs. The address of the hotel she gave me was

in a seedy neighborhood, the kind where drug deals take place in broad daylight. Every choice she makes is a clear indicator that the worst-case scenario is preferable to accepting my help.

Yes, it's a ding to my ego. But it cuts, too, damn it. I thought we were closer than this. Thought she trusted me. How many times had I told Diana that Aislinn was doing whatever it was she was doing for reasons we didn't know about yet?

"Sir?"

I nod to Paul, my driver. "Could you get the front door, Paul? I'll carry Miss Knightley."

I get out and circle around the limo, keeping an eagle eye out for photographers lurking behind parked cars or hidden in the shadows. But there's no one. A quiet, private neighborhood with gated trees and neighbors that include ambassadors, TV actors and investment bankers. When I decided to open my own firm, I bought the townhouse primarily for use by my clients—a secure getaway when they come to the city that offered quiet luxury and privacy. I thought of every detail, planned for every eventuality.

Not once did I think my personal life and some misguided, overly conservative opinions about dating would drag everything I've been working for to the brink.

I open the limo door slowly. Aislinn doesn't stir. I stare, relieved when her chest moves up and down. I lean down, unbuckle her, and gather her into my arms. She murmurs something and curls into my chest, her face resting once more against my neck, one hand wrapping around the hem of my jacket. My arms tighten around her.

I went after her because I was worried about her, yes, but also because she didn't give me a chance to dive deeper into how our marriage of convenience could benefit her, give her a start at a new life. Her facing down Marston had catapulted me back to that freezing winter afternoon when Aislinn and I had heard the snap of leather, followed by Diana's pained scream and a puppy's frightened yelp. The same rage, the same determination to stop whatever was happening by any means necessary.

But as I'd stalked across the hotel lobby, seen Aislinn lean in, shoulders thrown back and her spine straight, other emotions had reared their head. Fear. Admiration. And, most concerning of all, possessiveness. I'd seen the look in Marston's eye as he'd stared down at Aislinn. He wanted her. Just for that look alone, I could have punched him right in the face.

I walk up the stairs and shift Aislinn in my arms so that I can punch in the security code. Once inside, I tap the button to lock the door and go upstairs. The house boasts three bedrooms for clients who may have guests or family with them. But so far, I'm the only one who's used it, crashing in the master bedroom on late nights when I didn't feel like making the trek back to my penthouse. The first two bedrooms are unmade, but the last one, the one I've slept in, has fresh sheets, a clean blanket and a few amenities to make it feel more like a home.

I carry her in and lay her gently down on the bed. She stirs but doesn't open her eyes. I pull the blanket up over her and tuck the edges around her shoulders. I start to turn away, then freeze when her lips curve into a small smile. She inhales deeply, then releases a breath, as if she finally knows she's safe.

My hands clench into fists. Extreme emotional reactions after nearly a year of being separated from a woman who's like family to me. Of seeing her eviscerated in the media, abandoned by her adoptive parents and on the verge of losing everything.

Yes. That has to be it.

I'm at the door, my hand on the knob, when she breathes out a single word that stops me in my tracks.

"Liam."

My fingers clench down on the knob. I imagined it. Misheard it. Or even if I didn't, she's asleep. Whispering the name of the last person who helped her when she was losing control in a crowded room in front of prying eyes and flashing cameras. It means nothing.

I close the door behind me. Nothing.

I go back downstairs and turn on the light in my study before powering on my laptop. A couple minutes of research confirms that news of our engagement is everywhere.

Not how I pictured things playing out. But as I scroll through the pictures, the hastily written articles, the speculation in the comments, I can't help but smile. Most of the attention is positive, romantic, with writers and commenters fixated on my getting in-between Marston and Aislinn, carrying her out of the hotel. There's a few mentions of Dexter and his criminal activities, but it seems most outlets are following the lead of the initial article and highlighting how the FBI and DOJ's recent investigation cleared Aislinn of any wrongdoing.

Satisfied, I lean back in my chair. I imagined something more formal when it came to announcing our engagement. But this media coverage is good for both of us. In less than an hour, public opinion is already shifting in her favor.

My phone rings again. I frown when I see Eric's name pop up. Stephanie reached out several times over the last few months to see if Diana and I had talked to Aislinn. But Eric hadn't reached out. Not once.

The phone barely stops ringing when Eric texts me.

Where is she?

My jaw tightens. Eric saw what was happening to Aislinn, had to have known something was wrong when she started dating Dexter. When she fucking married him. How could he have missed how miserable she was?

Eric didn't protect her last time. Hell, I failed to protect her. But I'm not going to now. For better or worse, she and I are tied together for the foreseeable future. She's going to be pissed when she wakes up. But once she sees the media coverage, sees people are finally on her side, she'll see that this might be the best possible thing that could have happened.

I type back two words: With me.

Bubbles pop up showing he's typing a reply.

I switch my phone to silent and turn it over. I don't care what he has to say. As far as I'm concerned, he and anyone else who has hurt Aislinn can go to hell.

CHAPTER FIVE

Aislinn

Sunlight warms my skin. I snuggle deeper under a soft blanket and breathe in the delicious, sexy scent of cedar and spice.

Liam.

My eyes fly open as I sit up. I look around frantically. My heart jumps into my throat as I take in the unfamiliar surroundings. The huge bed with its mahogany frame. The thick navy blanket. The plush leather chair and ottoman tucked into an alcove and a stone fireplace where flames are crackling over several thick logs.

I blink and bite back my panic. It's been three months since my last panic attack. Three. I'm angry at myself that I lost control in a public setting, and in front of Liam, for God's sake. I'm not going to do that again. Especially when I don't know where I am.

I glance down and breathe a sigh of relief. I'm still in the same dress. There's no sign that anyone else has slept in the bed with me. This looks far too nice and homey to be a hotel. I distinctly remember telling Liam where I wanted to go last night, but after falling asleep, I remember nothing. Nothing but a sensation of being held. Of being safe.

I shake my head. This isn't Liam's penthouse on Billionaires' Row. As nice as his home in the sky is, it always felt more like Liam showing off his wealth than a place he could call home. This room, however, seems more like the kind of place he would enjoy. The paintings on the wall, mostly watercolors of the sea. I know he and his parents have spent a lot of time at a beach in Rhode Island. Water has always been calming for him. The colors seem like him, too: brown leather and dark wood trim with dark blue walls. Some might find it too dark, but it feels restful. Peaceful.

I can't remember the last time I would ever describe Liam as being peaceful.

Okay, stop. I need to stop psychoanalyzing the man I should not be in love with, especially after the ridiculous idea he proposed last night. Instead I need to focus on figuring out where I am, how I got here and what I'm going to do next.

I notice my phone lying on an end table. I reach over and grab it, frowning when it vibrates in my hand. I open the screen, and my mouth drops open. Dozens of text messages and numerous missed calls from Eric, Stephanie, coworkers I once considered friends…and Diana.

I press my lips together. I miss her. I miss her so much it hurts. But every time I think of her, I think of her hand tucked into the crook of Liam's arm. Think of the ring glittering on her finger. Feel the snapping of a connection I never thought could be broken. The severing of a friendship I once believed would withstand anything.

It's a pain I have to carry alone. Diana did nothing wrong. And while I can't stand the man Liam has become, with his twisted proposal and scheming to further his career, he had no idea his first engagement would crush me.

I scroll past Diana's texts and open one from Jamie, one of Eric's press assistants.

How did I not know you were dating Liam Whitlock? And now you're engaged?!

I freeze. Beneath the text is a screenshot from social media of Liam carrying me through the hotel lobby. There's a link. Slowly, I force myself to tap it. More pictures come up of Liam with his arm around my waist at the beginning of my panic attack, carrying me outside the hotel and trying to shield me from the cameras with his body. Liam setting me inside the limo.

I scroll through the text, the links. Shock turns into anger. I didn't like what Liam proposed yesterday. But going behind my back while I slept off a panic attack is something I never would have expected of him.

I sling back the blanket and scramble out of bed. My bare feet hit the floor. I stalk across the room and throw open the door. A quick search reveals no one on the second floor. In fact, there's no furniture in any room except the bedroom I was in.

Still angry and a little bit creeped out, I hurry down the stairs to the first floor. The scent of food hits me. My stomach growls. I don't even remember glancing at the time, but obviously it's the next day. The last time I ate was lunch. I couldn't stomach anything more than a couple of forced bites of appetizers at the gala last night.

I follow the scent toward the back of the house and step into the kitchen.

Liam is leaning casually against a granite top counter,

one long leg crossed over the other. He's dressed casually in a hunter green shirt, a trio of buttons undone at
the throat and the sleeves rolled up to his elbows, and a
pair of black jeans. Silver platters crowd the table next to
him. He has his phone pressed to his ear, but as soon as
he sees me, he ends the call.

"Good morning."

"You bastard."

One eyebrow arches up. "Not the greeting I was expecting."

"What did you expect?" I cross my arms over my chest.
"For me to just sit back and let you tell everyone we're
engaged while I'm sleeping off a panic attack?"

The air in the room drops ten degrees. Liam pushes
off the counter and starts walking toward me with slow,
measured steps.

I stand my ground. I'm not going to be intimidated
by him.

"Did you ever like me?"

The question takes me back. "What?"

"You think I'm capable of the most heinous acts." He
spits the words out, his voice sharp and lethal. "It's a wonder we were ever friends if this is what you thought I was
truly capable of."

Guilt tries to seep in, but I push it away. "The man I
used to know is not the man standing in front of me today.
The man standing in front of me," I say, "used what happened last night—"

"I did nothing. As you were sleeping across from me,
my phone started blowing up. They snapped compromis-
ing photos of us. Someone overheard our conversation
with Marston and told the press we were engaged."

There's no hint of lying in his gaze, no tell. The guilt

pushes back, hard. Am I being so hard on him because he deserves it? Or because I'm still angry? Hurt? "Okay," I say. "Have you tried to tell everyone it's not true?"

Liam grabs his phone, taps it a couple of times and hands it to me. It takes me a moment to focus on the words, to look past the photo of his body arched protectively over mine as he carries me out of the hotel. A dramatic photo. Both of us in black, with snowflakes swirling around us. No wonder it's getting so much press.

I continue scrolling, then stop. The title screams in all capital letters: Fairy Tale at Last for Innocent Victim, Government Criminal.

I scroll down farther. The story paints me as an innocent young woman seduced into marriage by an older man. It's the kindest portrayal I've seen of myself in the media since Dexter died. "Why do people care?"

I hate that my voice cracks. Hate that the words of a writer I've never met can make me feel something when I've spent so many months burying my emotions.

"Everyone loves a fairy tale," Liam said quietly. "You used to."

I scoff and shove his phone back at him. "I grew up. Just like you always said I should."

Silence falls. Slowly, I look up.

Liam is gazing at me with a tenderness that I have to consciously steel myself against. It's not romantic. It's not sweet. It's pitying. "I never meant like this, Aislinn."

"No. You were right. It was time to grow up." I look up at him. "Happily-ever-after is an illusion."

Liam's eyes sharpen. "What do you mean?"

Part of me wants to confide in him right then and there. To tell him how Eric looked the other way on just who was funding his first campaign, how he rubbed shoulders with men just like Dexter. Manipulated our country for their own financial gain and reputation.

Yet something holds me back. I don't owe Eric any loyalty, but I'm not quite ready to throw him to the wolves.

"I'm asking a lot of you," Liam says quietly. "But this arrangement will help us both."

"Why do you want to work for clients that dictate how you live your personal life?"

"Arthur Tarsney. William Luther. Anne Singleton. Know the names?"

A face appears in my mind. Sharp nose, dark gray hair combed back from a prominent brow. "I know Tarsney." He's been a generous donor to Eric's campaign over the years. Luxury real estate developer.

He's been a donor for over two decades. Is he one of the ones who bought votes with his support? Did he influence legislation so he could make more profit?

"And Luther," Liam continues, "is a former NASA engineer turned inventor with a patent on some of the latest technology being utilized by cell phone companies as they develop enhanced satellite systems. And Singleton took control of her husband's shipping company when he passed away in a car accident and turned it into an empire. They're the best."

"And you want to work with the best."

Liam has always wanted the best. I never begrudged him for it. How could I given the way he, Diana, and I grew up? But right now, it makes me sad. First it was getting into the best school for finance and accounting, then securing the best internship, and then a job with the most prestigious wealth management firm in the city. Now it's putting together his own management firm and having the wealthiest clients while owning a slate of New York's most impressive real estate.

Will any of it ever be enough?

"I'm the youngest investor in our firm's history to make partner. I took my own salary and turned it into a fortune nearing one billion dollars. I can do the same for my clients."

He speaks factually, earnestly.

"Then why does your dating life matter?"

"Luther's the one who brought up his concerns about what he referred to as my cavalier love life." His face darkens. "My accomplishments have been in a short amount of time. There's no longevity to back me up, and Luther, along with the others, have concerns that the way I've lived my personal life will be how I live my professional life. They want to see endurance, commitment."

"I'm sure Luther wasn't a saint back in the day."

"Back in the day, it doesn't matter because Luther was an engineer who wasn't under scrutiny by multimillion- and billion-dollar clients looking for an investor to manage their wealth. An investor they need to know won't back out of his obligations."

I open my mouth to argue, then decide what's the point? Liam's obviously ready to sell his commitment to bachelorhood for a chance to rub shoulders with snooty clients.

"Did you like everyone Eric did business with?"

The question is an arrow straight to my pride. "No."

"Did you still work with them?"

"Yes," I ground out.

"Being able to open up my own firm and have clients like Tarsney, Luther, and Singleton cement my firm's future. I owe it to…"

He stops himself, glances away. I frown, but before I can press, he turns back to me.

"This is what I want. This marriage can help us both. You read those comments. You won't have to sign off and start a new life somewhere. You can get your old life back or start a new legacy without always wondering if someone's going to recognize your name."

Oh, he's good. All the things I told myself I'd gotten over, that I no longer wanted, he's now offering to me on a silver platter. I still have no desire to go back and work for Eric. But to have my reputation back, to be able to figure out what I want to do with the rest of my life without constantly looking over my shoulder...

"Think about it while we eat." He nods to the table over my shoulder. "Before the food gets cold."

The very mention of food has my stomach growling again. Wincing, I glance back over my shoulder. My eyes widen as I take in the number of serving dishes. "What is all this?"

Liam moves around me and starts removing lids. Steam rises off a plate of thick omelets, with small bowls of chives and caviar sitting next to it. Oysters chill on ice. One platter hosts bagels sliced in half and piled high with smoked salmon, strips of red onion, capers and dill. Another offers sugar-coated donut bites with plump raspberries perched on the rim. There's a pitcher of mimosa with freshly sliced oranges resting on the surface and a coffeepot next to a plate of scones.

"Food."

I roll my eyes. "I can see that. Are you expecting company?"

"Just you." Liam grabs a plate and starts serving himself. "I ordered your favorites."

I blink rapidly as emotion wraps around my heart and squeezes. "The donut bites are from the bakery on the Upper West Side."

"Yes."

"But the omelets…that's from the restaurant on Roosevelt Island."

"Like I said, your favorites." As I stare at the food, Liam sets the plate down at the far end of the table and pulls out a chair. "Come sit."

His voice is gentle again, friendly. I respond to it before I can stop myself, placing one foot in front of the other as I cross the kitchen and sit down. I pick up my fork and cut off a small piece of omelet and force myself to eat slowly. It's hard when the omelet is cooked to perfection, savory with a hint of butter, when each bite is made all the more indulgent with the caviar and dill.

I keep my eyes on my food as Liam moves around the kitchen and fills his own plate. It's all so…ordinary. Domestic. Peaceful.

Liam will never love me. I know this. Will have to prepare myself for those moments when weakness will try to creep in. But the thought of having something like this, a calm friendship I can enjoy as I stitch myself back together, is no longer a simple temptation. It's something I desperately want.

CHAPTER SIX

Liam

"How long?"

I try, and fail, to suppress the triumph in my voice. "Five years."

She glares at me. "Two," she counters.

I lean back in my chair, pick up my glass of mimosa and smirk at her. I've been dealing in mergers and acquisitions for eight years. I know how to make a deal. "Five."

"This isn't one of your conference rooms."

Her retort, the fire in her voice, has me sitting up straight. This isn't the Aislinn I'm used to, the friend with the soft voice and kind smile who tries to make sure everyone is happy. No, this is a fiercer Aislinn, someone who won't back down.

"You need me." She points her fork at me, making me grateful we're sitting on opposite side of the table. "You're offering a good deal. But don't think for one second that I will not turn around and walk out the door if I don't like the terms."

The air between us shifts. Crackles. The attraction from last night rears its head, slams into me with a force

I can't ignore. My eyes drop down to her mouth, then back up to her mesmerizing eyes. For a moment, I imagine I see a similar desire in the familiar emerald—

Stop. I've always enjoyed verbally sparring with the women I've dated. Aislinn's newfound confidence is just intriguing.

"Four."

Before she can reply, her phone rings. Aislinn looks down at it and grimaces.

"Who is it?"

"Stephanie."

Her voice is resigned. But beneath I can hear the sadness, the bone-deep ache that comes from missing someone who's still here.

An ache I've fought off every day since Aislinn disappeared.

She starts to lay the phone on the table, then stops. "I should probably take this."

I think back to the way Stephanie's face looked the last time we talked, the fear and hopelessness as she tried to figure out why her daughter had distanced herself. "She'd like that."

Aislinn nodded and stood. I heard her faint "Hi, Stephanie" as she moved down the hall.

I prop my elbows on the table and scrub my hands over my face. From single to engaged—again—in less than twenty-four hours. The path had been choppier than expected, but I'd done it. Goal achieved.

But there was no satisfaction. No thrill of conquering the next step. No, right now all I felt was worry for my friend who had changed so drastically.

I stood and moved to the window. The snow was still falling, thick, heavy flakes that quickly piled on top of the branches outside. This corner of New York was quieter than most. With the snow smothering most of the sound, and obscuring my neighbors' homes from view, I could almost pretend I was back in the country.

Grief hit me hard and fast. Inevitable whenever I think about my parents. When I remember the early years spent in upstate New York, hot summers running through the fields along the river and winters spent cozied up by the fire watching Christmas movies and sipping on Mom's hot chocolate, I feel the twinges of a peace I haven't experienced in years. The comfort of Mom's hugs, the reassurance of Dad's deep, rumbling voice.

I still remember sneaking down one winter's night to look at all the presents piled under the tree and catching them stealing a kiss under the mistletoe, Mom's hand on Dad's cheek and his arms wrapped around her like he never wanted to let go. I'd had the usual *ick* response of any eight-year-old boy. But it had also made me feel… safe. I was lucky to have two parents who had wanted me, who told me whenever I asked that my birth mom had loved me so much, she'd given me a chance at a better life.

A life altered just six months after we moved to the city. A car racing too fast down a side street through a red light. Police at the door of our apartment in the middle of the night.

My fingers curl into fists at my side. The man who killed them is serving a long sentence for the crimes he committed that night. But it didn't bring them back. It didn't stop the deep, heart-wrenching ache as Child Services searched for any record of my birth mother or any family members and came up with nothing. It didn't change the fact that at age ten I was thrust from a loving, happy family into a system struggling to serve the hundreds of thousands of children in its care.

I glance back at the door. I can still hear the quiet murmur of Aislinn's voice. I would give anything right now to have Mom and Dad here with me, to tell me what to do to help her. I can't remember the last time I let myself remember, let myself feel.

But in this moment, I miss them so fucking much it takes everything inside me not to let out a yell of rage that life could be so cruel. Not just to me, but to two of the best people I've ever known.

My eyes flick over to my jacket hanging off the chair. I think back to the photo inside a small plastic bag. One Ari gave to me the last time he was in New York. A photo of the woman who had done even more than I could ever imagine; given up her life so I could have one. I haven't looked at in nearly two weeks, but I carry it around just the same. Some days it feels like a subtle way of honoring her. Other days it feels like penance. Logically I know her death isn't my fault. But that doesn't chase away the guilt.

The floor creaks behind me. I swallow the pain, the anger, and smooth out my face before I turn to face Aislinn.

My fiancée.

She's still in the damn dress, the one that makes a man think of sliding the straps down her arms and revealing more of her naked skin. Of watching it pool in a black silken heap at her feet before—

God, stop.

I mentally grasp onto other thoughts—finance reports, investment summaries, numbers and data—to stop the lust. Lust I have absolutely zero business feeling. If Aislinn agrees to this relationship, it will be strictly platonic.

I may be battling back a need I've never experienced before, but I'll be damned if I'm going to let it get in the way of rebuilding my friendship with Aislinn.

"Everything all right?"

She listlessly places her phone on the table. "As well as it can be, I suppose. She's worried about me, which is nice, I suppose." She sinks into her chair, and I follow suit, pouring her a tall glass of mimosa. She takes it and downs a good third of it.

"Careful now." I grin. "You'll be on the floor of the living room groaning about how the room is spinning before too long."

Her lips quirk at my reference to her first time drinking, when Diana and I made the mistake of taking our lightweight friend bar-hopping in SoHo for her twenty-first birthday.

I miss those years. Miss the casual ease of our friendship, the brightness of our futures. Miss when Aislinn was happy.

Aislinn sets her glass down on the table, folds her arms, and leans forward. "Now, as I recall, we were in the middle of a negotiation."

Blood hums in my veins at the challenge in her tone. I lean back in my chair and smile at her again. "Your move, Knightley."

Aislinn

"Three," I shoot back.

"Three and a half."

I bite down on my lower lip to prevent the reflexive

smile at his ridiculousness. I mentally calculate. In three and a half years, I'll be just over thirty. Three and a half years to get my life back in order, get myself financially stable. Then, maybe, I'll be in a good place to still pursue the one personal goal I have left.

"Three and a half. And while we're on terms," I continue, ignoring his smug smirk, "I'd ask that you keep any affairs as private as possible."

Liam's smile evaporates. His eyes narrow to slits. "Excuse me?"

"Not only would it hurt your persona, but I just don't feel comfortable—"

"I'm not going to be sleeping with other women while I have a ring on my finger." The disgust dripping from his voice has me looking down at my plate. "I have always been upfront with the women I've dated. My affairs have been brief, but I have never once been unfaithful."

I look down at the floor and suck in a deep breath. "I wasn't trying to insult you. I just didn't think that you would put your romantic life on hold for three and a half years."

"Well, think again." He pushes away from the table and stalks over to the window.

Once upon a time, I would have gotten up, too, laid a comforting hand on his shoulder, would have invited him to tell me what was wrong. But those times are long gone. Liam and I are both very different people now than we were almost a year ago.

"I expect the same of you," he snaps over his shoulder.

I take the shot. Yes, I don't like the way he's doing things, but I have no room to judge. And now, I'm a willing participant in his scheme.

God, I don't even recognize myself anymore. When

did I become this person? A schemer, a liar? The bright-eyed girl who met Liam and Diana all those years ago in the high school theater would be disgusted with the woman I've become.

"I'll be faithful," I say quietly.

His fingers knot into a fist at his side. "I'll have a bank account started for you. Deposits of—"

"No."

Liam glances back at me. "No?"

Now it's my turn to stand. "I'm not accepting payment to be your wife."

He opens his mouth as if to protest, then stops. "It won't be like it was with him."

I swallow hard. Liam and Diana could always read me. Not too hard when I always wore my heart on my sleeve. But it's just concerning to know, lately, he can still see me, still know me—even when there are so many days when I no longer know myself. "I just can't."

"An alternative suggestion then." He pauses, waits for my reluctant nod. "I know you have limited funds, but you have some. You won't have to worry about rent or utilities for the foreseeable future. Give me half and let me invest it for you."

I want to say no purely on principle. But Liam's talented. Otherwise, he wouldn't have caught the interest of someone like Arthur Tarsney. "All right."

Liam picks his phone back up and taps the screen. "Next Saturday?"

"For what?"

"Our wedding."

My throat constricts. "That soon?"

"Take advantage of the good press, start the count-down on our contract."

"And make sure I don't change my mind?"

"A consideration, yes."

I look away. It's all moving so fast. Just like last time. One day, I woke up happy, content. In the span of a couple of hours, I lost everything. My friends, the relationship I had with my adoptive father, my beliefs about the world. Everything, gone in an instant.

But I remind myself, Liam isn't Dexter. This arrangement is different. I'd be a fool not to take advantage of it. Maybe, just maybe, it'll change not only the public's perception of me but the people at the foundation. Maybe, after all this is through, I'll at least have some of what I've dreamed.

"Should we shake on it?"

Liam eyes my hand. "Given that we're going to have to kiss in front of people next week, maybe we should start practicing now."

My lip curls in disgust at Liam for suggesting it—and the desire that surges from my stomach straight down into my core at the thought of his mouth on mine. Can I do this? Separate myself enough to survive three and a half years married to Liam? I have to be. No time like the present to test myself.

"All right."

Surprise flares in Liam's eyes. He steps forward.

My pulse jumps. My breasts grow heavy. God, can he see how badly I've wanted this? How many nights I've dreamed of kissing him, the feeling of his hands on my skin—

My phone rings.

I look down. Eric. The sight of his name has the same effectiveness as someone dumping a bucket of ice water over me. My conversation with Stephanie had been...

hard. I miss her. Miss the relationship we had. The genuine concern in her voice had nearly undone me. I'd almost asked her.

But what if I was right, and she confirmed she'd been involved all along? Or, worse, what if she knew nothing about it, and I upended her life the same way Dexter had ruined mine?

Eric, though… I had no interest in talking to Eric. But I needed to get away from Liam. Needed space to breathe and think.

"I… I should get this."

I don't look at Liam as I hurry out over the kitchen. Wait until I get to the foot of the stairs before I hit Ignore. Eric will be furious, spouting off about image and damage control. What will the voters think of his adopted daughter getting engaged within a year of her husband passing? A husband who was a crook?

Takes one to know one, Eric.

But one good thing Eric's call did was interrupt that ridiculous moment in the kitchen. I hurry up the stairs and don't stop moving until I'm back in the bedroom with the door firmly shut behind me.

CHAPTER SEVEN

Aislinn

For the second time in a year, I'm staring at my reflection in a mirror and contemplating how different my wedding dress looks from what I'd always imagined for myself. When I married Dexter, I wore a tan sheath dress. I hadn't been bold enough to wear the black I'd wanted to, but tan had felt like a small middle finger to the man who had taken control of my life. The small satisfaction had carried me through the ceremony.

Today, though, I took a different tactic. I wanted a dress that would make me feel like a princess. More like my old self.

It's lovely, probably too opulent for a courthouse wedding. But when I saw it in the window of a gallery earlier this week, I couldn't resist sneaking back a few hours later to try it on. Taking a private car to the back alley entrance after hours had felt ridiculous, but it was a better alternative than giving the creeping vultures who seemed to photograph my every move these days a chance at seeing my wedding dress.

Worth it.

A full princess ball gown, with a bell-shaped skirt made of fluffy tulle and a sweetheart neckline decked with tiny jewels. The corset-like bodice adds a touch of sexiness, while the gauzy swaths of tulle that gently wrap over my upper arms feel like wings. The stylist I booked kept my makeup simple, my hair done in loose curls.

I smile slightly at my reflection in the mirror. For a moment, I see her—the old me. The one full of hopes and dreams and fairy-tale endings.

Then I raise my chin and see the woman I've become. Hard, cold, pragmatic. I have one dream I've held on to with an iron grip. But I've let everything else go, surrendered it to reality. There's strength, yes, but there's also a deep loneliness I've never experienced before. Not just from lack of friends or family, but a lack of…well, myself. I don't know who I am anymore. Don't know who I want to be. Right now, in this moment, that makes me feel the loneliest out of everything happening in my chaotic life.

I cut the cord on the pity party and rearrange one of the gauzy sleeves. At least today's ceremony will be cut and dry—a quick elopement in a courthouse just outside the city with two witnesses. Miles away from the prying eyes of the press, granting Liam and me the privacy we so desperately crave after our mutual turns in the spotlight.

Although, I think with a slight smile, hopefully I can ask someone to snap a photo of me with their phone. Even though marrying Liam is still not in my list of top choices, I like the way I look today. Years from now, this will be the moment I focus on. That for the first time in a very long time, I feel beautiful and hopeful. The future looks nothing like what I dreamed of so long ago. But it's far better than where I was just one week ago.

I shake my head. One week, yet it feels like a lifetime.

I spent most of my time at the brownstone out of sight of the cameras. Given that Liam will be officially opening the doors to Whitlock Investments a week after we return from our honeymoon, he's been gone most days and quite a few nights, too, finalizing licenses for his advisors and brokers, ensuring his agreements with banks and investment platforms and confirming his client list.

A list I overheard him saying on the phone now included his top three clients.

My humor disappears. Liam could have been a lot of things. But even from the first time I met him, he was always driven to succeed, to do better and be better. He told Diana and me a little about his adoptive parents. He also hinted that the foster homes he grew up in had been less than kind. Given his near-constant state of alertness, I had always assumed he'd experienced similar levels of abuse as Diana had. Yet he rarely talked about it. He always offered a listening ear, a teasing smile and a protective streak—whether Diana and I wanted it or not. But he always held himself back.

I do seem to have a knack for getting involved with emotionally unavailable people. Liam. Eric. My birth family.

I glance down at my dress. I have something new, obviously. I chose pale blue lacy underwear at the encouragement of the salesperson at the bridal boutique. Not that Liam will be seeing it. But I bought it for myself, not for him.

Still, I think with a touch of tightness in my throat, I'm missing the something borrowed. The something old. A parent beside me to walk me down the aisle.

The tightness shifts down, wraps around my heart as I fight back a sudden wave of tears. I wanted to ask Stephanie so badly to be here. But I can't. Not only would she ask if Eric could come, but I don't want to establish that connection again only to have it broken down the road. Broken when I learn she was involved or broken when she turns away from me for ruining the image she has of her husband.

I raise my chin. I was always told by my foster care parents how sweet I was, how if they were in a place to adopt me, they would. I clung to those words, to that hope, throughout my childhood. I knew life wasn't perfect, but I was fortunate to have kind families who genuinely supported me, who helped keep that hope alive. A hope Stephanie and Eric had validated when they'd adopted me.

But I know better now. Pinning my hopes and dreams on others does nothing but leave room for disappointment and heartache. When I depend on myself, I can make my own way.

I refocus on the mirror. I have three and a half years to plan and prepare for that dream. Today, though, I need to focus on getting through this ceremony. I turn one way, then the other. Doubt creeps in. Is it too much? Did I really need to purchase an actual wedding dress?

Yes.

Even if I'm nervous, even if there's that nasty weak streak in me that wants Liam to like it, I wanted to wear this for myself. I won't marry again. Two loveless marriages are enough in one lifetime. But if this is going to be my last wedding, I'm going to look good walking down that aisle.

A knock sounds on my door. I frown. Liam said he was traveling ahead to the courthouse to make sure everything was ready and the security detail was in place. Did he forget something?

"Yes?"

"It's me. Diana."

I never thought it possible to have one's heart jump and sink at the same time. I swallow past the sudden thickness in my throat and smooth my hands over the tulle skirt as I walk to the door. I grab the knob, whisper a quick prayer and open it.

"Aislinn!" Diana's smile is so bright it nearly blinds me. I blink, unsure of what to say, but she beats me to it by letting out a very Diana-like squeal. "You look so beautiful." She starts to reach for me, then pauses. Uncertainty flickers across her face.

I debate for less than a second before I step forward and hug her.

Her arms come around me, and she crushes me to her. "I missed you, Aislinn."

I have to fight to keep the tears at bay. "I missed you, too."

She squeezes me one more time before leaning back and sweeping me from head to toe with her shining eyes. "This is such an amazing dress."

She doesn't seem jealous or upset. But I'm still not sure what to say, what to do. How to feel as I stand in front of one of my best friends in the dress I'll wear to marry her ex-fiancé. "Thank you."

Her eyes come back up to mine. She frowns. "Are you all right?" She lays a hand on my arm. "Are you sure you should be doing this?"

I pull away and walk over toward a window. Even though she's engaged to Liam's brother, does she still have feelings for Liam? Or, like so many in my life, does she have a mean streak I never saw and just doesn't want her ex to be with someone else? "I can only imagine how hard this is on you."

"What?"

"My being engaged to your ex-fiancé."

Silence reigns behind me. Each passing second feels like a sharp needle pricking my skin. Then, finally, "Did Liam not tell you?"

"No. I…no."

Diana lays a gentle hand on my arm and turns me around. I should have let Liam tell me whatever happened between the two of them. Shouldn't have put it off so that I'd be finding out all the heartbreaking details the morning of my wedding—

"The engagement was fake."

My brows draw together. "What?"

Diana rolls her eyes. "Looks like I'm not the only one who doesn't share."

Confused, I frown and repeat, "What?"

Diana waves her hand in the air. "Nothing. Long story, and one best told over a glass of wine. Preferably a big, big glass."

"Yeah, but… I don't understand." Anger creeps in. Liam told me his and Diana's engagement had nothing to do with the controversy with his clients. Did he lie to me?

Diana runs a hand through her thick, dark hair. "I'll tell you anything you want to know. I don't know how much you want to hear about Dexter on your wedding day."

"You know why Liam and I are getting married, right?"

"I do. It doesn't change the fact that today is still your wedding day, and unlike before, you and Liam care about each other."

My whole body goes on alert. "Care?" I repeat.

"I know the three of us haven't been close lately. But a friendship like ours isn't one that just fades away after a few months."

I breathe out. "No, I suppose not. Still, I'd like to know. I've been worrying that my getting engaged to him so soon after your broken engagement might hurt you. So hearing what actually happened would be helpful."

Diana winces. "Sorry. I didn't think about that. Although…" She hesitates again. "It has to do with Dexter."

The mention of his name doesn't hit as hard as it used to. There's still an unpleasant twinge, sometimes a flash of his face in my mind. But compared to my skin breaking out in a sweat and glancing over my shoulder for a solid hour afterward, I've made huge strides. "I need to know."

Diana nods and moves toward the window. "Shortly after you and Dexter were married, Liam ran into him. I forget where, but Dexter accused Liam of being in love with you."

The ground drops out from under me. I stand, immobilized by a torrent of emotions I can't even begin to unpack. "He what?" I finally croak out.

"And Dexter was convinced that the two of you were secretly in love and that Liam might one day try to make a move, initiate an affair or even convince you to leave Dexter."

I start laughing. I laugh until my sides hurt, and I wonder if I'm going to split the stitches of my dress. It's either laugh or cry.

"Aislinn?"

I wipe away a couple of tears. "Dexter is even more of an idiot than I thought he was if he thought that Liam was interested in me romantically."

Diana cocks her head to one side.

I turn and look out the window, not wanting to risk the possibility of her seeing my feelings for Liam reflected in my eyes.

"The way you say that makes me feel like you don't think you're good enough for him."

I shake my head. "One, Liam is like a brother to me, and I'm like a sister to him. Always have been, always will be. Two, once upon a time, I wanted marriage and kids and fidelity. A commitment. You and I both know Liam loves and accepts who he is. The things I want out of life, or wanted, are not the things he does."

"Okay." Diana doesn't sound completely convinced, but she lets it go. "For whatever reason, Dexter thought there was something there. He threatened Liam and you and me."

My head snaps around. "What?"

"So Liam decided to cover his tracks by saying that he was already engaged. He used me as the fake fiancée, partially to protect me because we were friends and he thought we could pull it off, and because a part of him was hoping that the shock of your two best friends suddenly getting engaged would encourage you to reach out."

God, Dexter had all of us dancing to his tune. So many threats, so many threads in his web that we could all barely move without getting caught.

A heavy knot of guilt settles in the pit of my stomach. I was so abrupt to them at the funeral, ignored all of Diana's texts over the last few months. All because I was angry. I never once thought myself capable of this. But when I look at the actions I've taken over the last year, when I think back to the secrets I've concealed all in the name of the greater good, the people I've shut out of my life, I don't even recognize the woman I've become. And now, learning that Liam and Diana were just trying to protect me gouges a far deeper wound in my heart than Dexter could have ever inflicted.

A red cardinal flies into view and lands on a snow-covered branch just outside the window, a flash of red against stark white. I stare at it, keeping my gaze focused outward as I speak. "I was so angry and hurt when I saw the two of you at Dexter's funeral. I had no right to be, but I was."

"Why?"

Because I thought you were engaged to the man I've loved for twelve years. I don't think I'll ever be able to tell her the whole truth, so I settle for bits and pieces of it.

"I had thought after the funeral the three of us might be able to reconnect. I had no right to feel betrayed, but there had been so much change, and that was the final straw. At the end, I didn't know how, even if I did reach out, our friendship would survive." I grimace. "That probably seems unfair with Liam and I now being engaged, but this is different. It's just two friends helping each other out." I finally suck up enough courage to turn and face her. "I understand if this affects—"

Diana holds up a hand. "Don't. One day, I will need to know what happened. With you leaving, your marriage, all of it. But today is not that day." She holds my gaze. "Are you sure you want to do this? Liam can be very persuasive, and I know a part of me felt like I had to say yes when he asked me to be his fake fiancée after everything he's done for me over the years. I don't want that for you."

"I didn't at first," I admit. "But I know this will help Liam. It feels deceptive, but I also don't agree with his clients pressuring him and monitoring his personal life. And," I add quietly, "people are enjoying the story. It feels like one giant lie, but no one has supported me since Dexter died. I want the chance to have a new life."

"Then I'm here for you. I'm here for you," Diana repeats as she lays a hand on my shoulder.

I blink rapidly. "Thank you."

"You're welcome. Now," she adds with a big smile, "Time to get you to your wedding."

Nerves flutter in my stomach as Diana walks across the room. She stops and glances back, frowning when she sees me still standing by the window.

"Aislinn, you don't have to—"

"I'm fine." I force out a tight-lipped smile. "Truly. This is what I want."

We both know I'm lying. I want the benefits from this arrangement, not the marriage itself. The initial relief I felt at knowing Liam and Diana's engagement was fake is gone. It was so much easier to keep myself emotionally distant, to be angry, when I thought they'd gotten engaged out of love. Knowing they did it for me opens up the door to all the feelings I spent the past four months burying.

I was strong enough to survive Dexter. But am I strong enough to survive three and a half years married to the man my heart won't let go of?

I glance down at the solitaire diamond on my finger. The sunlight catches it, casting sparkles onto the wall.

I made a promise. I'll keep it. The rest is mine to deal with.

I nod to Diana, more confident than I feel. "Let's go."

A sleek black car is waiting outside. A chauffeur opens the door and helps bundle the billowing skirts of my gown inside.

"How long until we get there?" Diana asks as the car pulls away from the curb.

"Twelve minutes, ma'am."

"Twelve minutes?" I frown. The courthouse is at least twenty minutes away, and that's in good traffic.

"We're not going to the courthouse," Diana tells me.

"Oh?"

Diana reaches over and squeezes my hand. "It's a surprise."

I once loved surprises. They didn't have to be big or extravagant. Something as simple as Stephanie showing up with my favorite latte could brighten any bad day. But the last time someone told me I was getting a surprise, Dexter had his hand wrapped around my neck like a vice and was dragging me out of the back of the car onto a California beach.

Diana gives me another reassuring squeeze. "It's a good surprise. I promise."

CHAPTER EIGHT

Aislinn

THE CAR WINDS its way through New York. The city is always busy, but a little less frantic on Saturday morning as the snow deafens the noise; it makes everything seem cleaner, brighter. Lights glimmer in the windows of cafés and storefronts. Towers and skyscrapers reach up and disappear into the low-lying clouds. People walk along the sidewalks, dressed in bright pops of color. Red, blue, even a pink-and-white-striped winter coat with a matching pink hat. So many details I used to enjoy. So many things I haven't paid attention to in the last few months. It was easier to shut out the world, draw into myself.

Yet as I watch the world pass by, I realize how much I've missed it.

That cautious ray of hope, the same one I felt the morning of Dexter's funeral when I saw Liam and Diana in line, flickers to life. Part of me wants to squelch it.

But as I glance over at Diana, then back out at the people on the streets, I find myself wanting just a little bit more. I can never go back to the way I lived my life before. I've seen too much to believe the world is a rosy, happy place. But maybe I can find a middle ground, a place in between where I can enjoy bits of happiness and small victories. Or I can find some good in this arrangement with Liam while still keeping my heart safe.

I glance down at the engagement ring on my left hand. Delicate bands of silver twine over one another like the branches of a tree to the center of the ring, where an oval-shaped diamond glitters between two drops of emeralds. Sweet and delicate. Liam surprised me at breakfast three days after we agreed to an official engagement. I was going stir-crazy from being cooped up. He'd dropped to one knee in front of my chair and popped open the lid on a deep blue velvet case to reveal the stunning ring. And damn my heart, it had shot into my throat faster than a shooting star.

Got to do at least one thing traditionally. He'd said it with a small smile as he slid the ring onto my finger. And then he stood, kissed me on the forehead like a brother would a little sister and left.

I curl my hand into a fist and turn it to the side so I can't see the ring.

The car turns onto Billionaires' Row, then makes another turn into the private parking garage.

"Are we going to Liam's penthouse?"

Diana shakes her head. "Nope."

A few minutes later, we're in a secure elevator racing up toward the sky. I watch the numbers, my confusion growing as Diana presses the button for the one hundred and thirty-first floor, several floors above where Liam's penthouse is.

"Friends in high places?" I joke.

Diana chuckles. "Something like that."

As the elevator ascends, I glance once more at my

friend. She's always been beautiful. But now she's glowing. There's a contentment about her, a peace I never saw. A far cry from the woman who befriended me in a high school theater, who held on to my hand like it was a lifeline as she lay in a hospital bed after suffering through an attack no child should ever experience. She was so brave, but she shouldn't have had to be. She should have been cared for, loved.

My eyes slide down to the ring on her finger. "You're happy?"

Diana glances at me, startled. Then a smile comes over her face, so bright and happy it brings tears to my eyes.

"You love him?"

Diana nods. "I do. More than I ever thought possible."

I hesitate. Then, quietly, "Maybe at the end of our honeymoon, we could have that big glass of wine."

Diana's eyes are shining as she reaches over and hugs me again. "I'd really like that. You're going to love Iceland, too."

I'd been surprised when Liam had suggested Iceland for our honeymoon. But I'd never been, and knowing his birth mother and brother were born and raised there, it seemed like a good location for both of us. He's arranged for a couple days in Reykjavik, including a few dinners at some high-end restaurants and even a visit to the opera house for a ballet performance, before we head north for a quieter stay at a remote villa.

I frown. Every time I've tried to get Liam to talk about his brother or his birth mother, he changes the subject. Just like he used to whenever Diana or I would ask about his childhood before foster care or his adoptive parents. We learned quickly that those were topics not even we were privy to. Something Diana had accepted, but something that, despite my best intentions, had hurt.

Apparently, I think with a quiet sigh, some things haven't changed. Liam wants to know all about my time with Dexter, my ugly, painful secrets, while he gets to keep his hidden away.

Another reason, I remind myself, to not let myself think this arrangement can be anything permanent.

At last, the elevator stops. Floor one hundred and-thirty-one. The top of the tallest building in New York. I mentally rack my brain. I can't remember who owns this.

The doors open to reveal a two-story living room. Diana and I walk out, the elevator doors closing quietly behind us. I walk across the floor to the window. On a clear day, I'd be able to see not only New York but the ocean and the surrounding states. Right now, though, clouds blanket the city. Only the tallest skyscrapers are visible.

"Welcome."

I turn, then do a double take. I know intrinsically the man walking into the room isn't Liam. Just a touch taller and slimmer, with white-blond hair instead of Liam's dark brown. But the face, the sharp blade of his nose, the chiseled cheekbones and angular jaw... He could be Liam's twin.

He doesn't notice me. He only has eyes for Diana. He crosses the room to her, his arms going around her waist and pulling her against him before he covers her lips with his in a passionate kiss.

I stare for a moment before embarrassment floods me, and I turn back to the window. Beneath the embarrassment, envy pumps through me. Sick, ugly poison. I bite down on my lower lip. After everything Diana has been through, how can I possibly be jealous that she has found someone to love and respect her? To cherish her?

"Aislinn?"

I swallow hard, get myself under control, then turn and face Liam's brother.

"Ari, this is Aislinn." The pure joy in Diana's voice makes me want to sink into the floor.

"Hello."

Ari smiles at me. "So you're Aislinn?"

"I am. Yes." Flustered, I thread my fingers together in front of me. "I know this is probably awkward—"

"Not at all." He crosses to me and holds out a hand. I shake it. "Diana and I are used to the unconventional. I'm glad that you and Liam are able to help each other out." His eyes narrow slightly. "As long as you're sure this is what you want."

I can't help but let out a small chuckle. "I take it you also have a protective streak?"

"I may have only known Liam for a few months, but in that time, I've come to discover how persuasive he can be." His indulgent smile dims as his voice softens. "And you've been through a lot."

The simple acknowledgment touches me. "Thank you. And I appreciate you asking, but I do want this."

"All right. Well, if you're ready, Liam is waiting for you."

Warmth flows through me. *It's an illusion*, I remind myself. *None of it's real.* "All right."

"You look beautiful."

I smile at Ari. "Thank you."

Diana and I follow Ari. He leads us out a glass door onto a stone terrace. Snow swirls around us. We walk around a corner, and my eyes widen. A huge greenhouse takes up this portion of the terrace. Behind the glass is another world, bright blooms and exotic trees.

We walk into a small vestibule. Ari closes the door behind us, waits a moment and then, at the sound of a soft bell, opens another door into the greenhouse. Warm, fragrant air rushes over me. I shrug out of my coat as I stare around in wonder. Huge, fuchsia-colored blooms drip from a bougainvillea tree. Other flowers, ones I've never seen before, show off a stunning array of colors. Violet, burgundy, deep jewel tones throw us into a world of summer.

"Where are we?"

"A secret garden."

My head snaps up. Liam is standing just a few feet ahead on a stone path, legs spread and hands tucked into his pockets. He looks so incredibly handsome. Black tuxedo tailored perfectly to his broad shoulders and thick arms. I've never been a fan of bow ties, but Liam wears his with masculine confidence. He's smiling at me, cocky and proud.

"A secret garden," I repeat.

"Your favorite book."

My lips part. "You remember that?"

"Every time I'd find you in the library or the food court or out on the green, you always had that book with you."

No. No, no, no. He can't do this. I don't want him to make me feel special. I don't want him to make me feel anything. I wrench my gaze away from him. My heart's pounding so fast it's making me lightheaded. "So we're getting married here?"

"Is that all right?"

The thread of concern underlying his words makes me

look back. He's watching me, the smile still in place. But there's something else in his eyes. Worry.

For a friend. Just a friend.

Like the time he brought Diana and me coffee at two in the morning when we were both cramming for exams. Like the numerous times he walked Lucy, Diana's dog, when she got caught late at her internship. Like the time I brought a birthday cake to the wealth management firm where he was interning because he couldn't get off. He's doing what friends do. Remembering the little things and caring for each other.

"Yes. Thank you."

"You're welcome." He gestures down the path. "Shall we?"

"Coats first." Diana fans her face. "It's hot in here."

Ari moves behind her and helps her out of her coat. She kept it simple with a long, black evening gown, but she still looks like a dark-haired goddess. Judging by the way Ari's eyes flare, he's imagining what she looks like out of it as he sets the coat down on a bench near the door. He holds out his arm and smiles at Diana as he escorts her down the path.

My lips quirk as I slide mine off. The sound of a sharp inhale has me looking up.

Liam is staring at me. His blue eyes are hot, flames burning bright as his gaze travels up and down my dress. I stand, immobilized by my own desire and wonder. I can feel his stare as if it were his fingers instead of his smoldering eyes on me. I press my thighs together, but it doesn't stop the heat. Thank God the bodice is thick. Otherwise everyone would be able to see my nipples hardening, pressing against the fabric.

Liam's gaze snaps back up to mine. Beneath the currents of lust pulsing between us is something new: awareness. I've always admired Liam from afar. Ached for him in a romantic sense, the way I imagine Jane Austen heroines pining for their loves. But this sensual need is different. Incredible.

Terrifying.

Apparently, Liam has the same thought because the desire vanishes as quickly as it appeared. "Ready?"

His voice is still friendly, his face relaxed and open. But as I set my coat down on the bench and move toward him, I see the tightness in his jaw, the blankness in his eyes. I'd be lying if I said I didn't feel just a bit more beautiful. Powerful. Even sexy.

But his ability to turn off his emotions, to shut me out as quickly as he just did, is just another sign. No matter how much I may care for him, no matter how attractive I find him, we'll never be compatible. I want a family, children. He doesn't.

Once I'm free of this marriage, I'll create my own family. Follow through on all the vague promises of my former foster parents and adopt children who deserve a loving home. A decision I know Liam and Diana will both support, especially given the far harsher experiences they both had in foster care.

But not something Liam wants for himself. And even if he did, even if we were compatible, I don't think I can ever trust myself to be in a committed relationship again.

I almost laugh. For once, Liam and I have the same goal; to never get married to anyone else. Never let ourselves fall in love. That, coupled with my feminine satisfaction at knowing Liam at least finds me attractive, too, gives me a much-needed boost of confidence.

"Yes."

Liam holds out his arm. I slide my hand into the crook of his elbow, focusing on the incredible foliage around me instead of the feel of his arm beneath my fingers.

A stream winds its way through the flowers. The soft babbling of the water feels like sinking into a hot tub after a long day. When a bird flies overhead, I can't help but laugh. This bit of summer in the midst of a New York winter is incredible.

Liam's arm tenses beneath my fingers. I glance up to see him looking down at me with a small smile.

"What?"

"I haven't heard you laugh in a long time."

"It's been a while." I give his arm a gentle squeeze. "Thank you."

The path curves past a tree with rambling roots and moss hanging from its rugged branches. Just beyond the tree is a stone patio. Huge pink blooms have been threaded through a wooden arch. Diana is standing on the bride's side with two matching bouquets in her hands. Ari is on the groom's side, chatting quietly with a young woman in a black dress and an older man in a white shirt and tan slacks.

"Our officiant and a photographer," Liam murmurs. "They're unaware of our agreement."

I push back the spurt of guilt. We're not marrying for love. But we are marrying. We're committed to the arrangement. I'm sure it's not what Liam's archaic-minded, high-and-mighty clients had in mind, but it shouldn't matter anyway.

That above all else helps me slip into my public relations mode as the older man glances over his shoulder. He has a craggy, well-worn face, with a square jaw and lines carved deep into his forehead.

"Liam." He walks over and holds out his hand to me, a big smile on his face. "And you must be Aislinn."

"Yes." I return his smile. "Thank you for officiating our ceremony… I'm sorry, I didn't catch your name."

"Bill. And it's my honor." His smile deepens. "Never thought when I got certified to officiate my daughter's wedding a few years ago I'd have the chance to use it again."

"Well, thank you."

"Of course." His eyes are kind as he gestures toward the arch. "I hope this is to your liking."

This time there's no pretending. "It's beautiful." I steal a quick glance at Liam, give him a small smile. "Just like a secret garden." I look away before I let myself feel too much. "I can't thank you enough for making this possible."

Bill looks back and forth between Liam and me. He almost looks satisfied.

Odd.

"Normally it's just my wife and myself who make use of it. My daughter lives in Portugal and my son is away at college in London. It's nice to have people here again." He looks back at Ari, Diana and the photographer. "We're ready if you are."

As ready as I'll ever be. I keep my eyes on Bill as I nod. "I'm ready."

I walk up to the arch with Bill and Liam. Diana hands me my bouquet, gives me a hug and then my second wedding begins.

The photographer is good. Aside from the quiet clicking of her camera, I barely notice her as Bill talks. I stare at Liam, my fingers clenching and unclenching around the stems of my bouquet. Thankfully the large petals hide my knuckles. Otherwise I'm sure everyone would see how white they are.

"And now the vows."

Diana gently nudges me. I turn and hand her my bouquet, trying to look calm before I turn back to Liam. I brace myself as he takes my hands in his.

"Liam, do you take Aislinn to be your lawfully wedded wife, to have and to hold from this day forward, for better or worse, for richer or poorer, in sickness and in health, to love and to cherish until death do you part?"

Or three point five years from today.

"I do."

His voice is a gentle, familiar rumble. I remember the first time I heard it in the high school theater. The kind of play we're acting out now, though, has far higher stakes for both of us.

I squeeze his hands and give him a small smile. He blinks, a tiny furrow appearing between his brows. I hold his gaze as I repeat my vows.

"The rings?"

Ari hands Liam the rings. Liam hands me a thick silver band, which I carefully slide onto his finger. He slides a matching slimmer one onto my finger, the same woven bands of silver holding tiny diamonds in their grasp. A perfect match for the engagement ring.

At least this time I'm not stuck with an ostentatious jewel that could be seen from space. I like the simplicity, the casual elegance.

"I now pronounce you husband and wife. You may kiss the bride."

You can do this, you can do this, you can do this.

I freeze. Do I put my arms around his neck? Do I lay my hands on his shoulders? How does one kiss one's best friend and make it look like I care while hiding the fact that I actually do care?

My mind's spinning. I know it is. I'm so focused on making it stop that when Liam slides an arm around my waist and pulls me close, I simply relax into him. My hand automatically comes up to rest on his shoulder. The other settles on his chest. His very muscular chest.

Heat floods my body. Startled, I look up just as his hand settles on my cheek in a gentle cradle that makes my lip part.

And then he's kissing me. Liam, one of my best friends and the only man I've ever loved, is kissing me. I stay still, not wanting to do anything wrong, not wanting to give any hint of how much this simple touching of mouths is making my body so hot I can barely stand it.

Until Liam's lips part. My mouth responds. The sudden intimacy of it, of sharing breath as his fingers firm on my cheek and his arm tightens about my waist, as he *groans* into my mouth, turns the heat into a raging wildfire.

It's a good thing I've already committed to never getting married again. Because no kiss will ever top this.

Then just like that, it's over. Liam pulls away. He smiles down at me, his eyes still that same blue blankness from just before we walked down the path. The camera clicks, the sound now like a gunshot as I remember.

That wasn't a real kiss. It was theater.

Bill, Diana and Ari approach us, offering congratulations and thankfully giving me a reprieve from looking at Liam.

My husband.

I ignore Diana's concerned frown and Ari's speculating gaze as we all make small talk about the wedding, the honeymoon, our plans for when we return to New York.

If they think there's the possibility of something romantic between Liam and me, then we're off to a good start with this farce of a marriage.

A chill creeps over my skin. I glance down at the engagement ring, now joined by the wedding band. It's strange how such slender pieces of jewelry can suddenly feel so heavy.

CHAPTER NINE

Liam

I GLANCE OUT my window as the plane soars over the Labrador Sea. There's nothing but a star-speckled sky above and a dark blue carpet thousands of feet below.

As I reach for my old-fashioned, my ring clinks on the glass. It feels strange, cold. Even knowing there's an expiration date for wearing it, it doesn't negate the tightness around my finger, the heaviness pressing on my skin.

My gaze slides over to where Aislinn is seated on the opposite side of the plane. We've barely said ten words to each other since we boarded. She changed out of her wedding dress into a long-sleeved navy shirt and wide-legged burgundy pants. Her golden hair is tucked behind her ears, her eyes focused on her laptop screen in front of her.

Aislinn. One of the few people in this world I trust. My friend.

My wife.

My chest tightens. When she took off her coat, I nearly swallowed my tongue. The billowing skirt reminded me of a princess. Sweet, romantic, just like Aislinn used to be. But the top of her dress...just thinking about the way the fabric clung to her slender waist, the dip in the front that teased me with a view of the swells of her breasts, the see-through scraps of fabric draped over her arms, made me hard in an instant. I've never really noticed a woman's shoulders before. But I noticed Aislinn's, noticed her bare skin, imagined what it would be look to kiss her there as I slid the bodice down and lowered my head to her—

Fuck, stop.

I look back out the window, my hand clenched around my glass. What the hell is wrong with me? I've always thought Aislinn was beautiful. But ever since that first night at the gala when I saw her in the black dress, I've been cursed by an awareness of her as a woman. A stunning, sensual woman who is far stronger and confident than I ever realized.

Yet she's holding back. This entire last week, every time we talked, she was distant. Muted. When she laughed in the greenhouse, when I saw her smile, it was like finally being able to take a deep breath for the first time in over a year.

There you are.

The old Aislinn, the one who loves fairy tales and greeted everyone by name and played hide-and-seek with kids in Central Park simply because they asked her to, is still in there. She's just buried herself so deep no one can get to her.

I bite back a smile. I have three and a half years to find out what happened. To help Aislinn get out of this hole she's hiding in. To do what I should have done last year and fight for her.

Fight for her, not kiss her.

The blend of bourbon, bitters and a dash of sugar is smooth, sweet. I focus on the scent of orange, the glimmer of light through the caramel-colored drink. Anything but the way Aislinn felt in my arms. The way she tasted.

God, she tasted good.

I can't think this way. Can't let Aislinn in this way. I'm much more of a coldhearted bastard than I realized, enjoying my friendship with her even as I kept parts of myself concealed. Worse, when I think about how Aislinn opened herself up and let me in from the very beginning. It was one of the things that drew me to her, that dauntless kindness and trust. How even after years of not having her dreams fulfilled, she still thought the world was good.

And I took everything she offered without hesitation.

Disgusted with myself, I stare at the curled orange rind artfully arranged in my glass. It's not just my heart I want to protect. It's hers, too. She deserves far more than my selfish self can give her.

I set the glass down harder than I intend. It clinks on the hardwood of the table and sloshes up over the rim. I curse as Aislinn glances up with a frown.

"Everything all right?"

I give her a tight smile. "Yes. Just clumsy."

She nods and turns back to her computer, which just pisses me off even more. I saw the way she looked at me when she first took off her coat in the greenhouse. She felt something, too. I know desire when I see it; Aislinn found me just as attractive as I found her. But she had no problem switching it off.

Which is a good thing.

Maybe if I repeat it enough times, I'll stop gritting my teeth at the memory of her lips parting beneath mine. Of wishing I had had just a moment longer to feel her body pressed against mine.

I suck in a deep breath. Which is a mistake because somehow I inhale the scent of spiced rose.

I stand and stalk toward the galley at the front of the plane. When I reserved the private jet, it seemed like a good idea to both keep prying eyes at bay and continue to sell the secret romance that's been so popular. I just hadn't anticipated it turning into a private hell of my own making.

I reach the galley. Light gray cabinets, green quartz countertops and soft lighting give the kitchen a cozy feel. The size of it rivals the kitchen I had in my first apartment. Two attendants are moving about, pulling pans out of the oven and arranging food on plates.

"Mr. Whitlock."

One of the attendants smiles at me. Kacey, I remember. Long red curls pulled back with a clip, a big smile and huge green eyes. A year ago, I would have flirted. If she'd flirted back, I would have invited her to dinner, drinks, a night in whatever hotel I was staying in.

Now it's like looking at a painting. I can acknowledge she's beautiful. Yet I feel nothing. Not even a flicker of attraction. It's odd, but I'm grateful for it. Three and a half years of celibacy will be interesting. But I meant what I said to Aislinn. I have never been unfaithful, and I never will be, even if our marriage is a business arrangement.

"Just stretching my legs."

"Understandable, sir. Dinner will be served in five minutes."

I walk back to the main cabin. Aislinn is still on her computer, oblivious to the world around her.

"Shopping?" I ask as I sit back down.

"Job hunting."

I frown. "Already?"

"Yes." She shakes her head. "More like reapplying."

"For?"

Her eyes flick to me. She hesitates, then lets out a long sigh. "Working for the Foster Foundation."

I snort. "They should be begging you to come work for them."

She gives me a sad smile. "Thanks."

Warning bells clang. I keep my voice cautious, my tone even as I pick up my glass again. "What happened?"

Her walls are thankfully down, allowing me to see the debate playing out across her face. Once she would have told me everything. Now it's like prying a favorite toy away from a child to get her to share just a small piece of her life.

"I knew last month that continuing to work for Eric wouldn't be a good idea. He hadn't said anything yet," she adds as my hand tightens around my armrest, "but I knew. So I started applying for other jobs. One of them was for a director of public relations with the Foster Foundation."

"They rejected your application because of Dexter."

At her nod, I grab my phone.

"What are you doing?"

"Contacting one of their board members." I pull up my contacts. Anger seethes inside me. After everything Aislinn has done for kids in foster care, all of the attention she's brought to the Foster Foundation and other organizations, and they reject her because of her ass of a husband?

"Don't." Her voice whips out.

Slowly, I turn my head. She's gripping her armrests, as if physically restraining herself from jumping out of her seat to stop me.

"I'm just trying to help."

"And I didn't ask you to."

"No," I reply coldly. "Because you don't need help anymore, do you?"

A lock of hair falls from behind her ear. She tucks it back with a violence that seems to surprise her as she slowly leans back in her seat. "I'm not trying to be ungrateful, Liam." Now her voice is calm, almost eerily so. "I just want to do some things for myself for once. I don't need my husband taking charge again."

Ice sinks into my skin. Slowly, I tuck my phone into my pocket and pick up my glass.

"Liam." Her heavy sigh fills the cabin. "That wasn't—"

"Comparing me to Dexter?" I swirl the contents of the glass before taking a long drink. "Good."

Except we both know that's exactly what she was implying.

Silence falls between us. For the second time that day, I question whether this marriage was a good idea or not. The reason this time, however, is not my inconvenient physical attraction to a friend. It's my wife's continuous reminders that she has a low opinion of me.

I let down my guard with Aislinn and Diana. Not completely. But more than I have with anyone else since Mom and Dad died. I spent months digging for information on Dexter, first to find out why Aislinn had chosen him and then to help her as she faced down public opinion on her involvement in Dexter's crimes. Every time Diana wondered if Aislinn had simply changed, I defended her. Every time a newspaper article or news report questioned whether or not Aislinn had been involved, I dug deeper.

No more. She wants to compare me to her manipulative dick of a husband, fine. But I'm not going to waste any more time trying to help her. Hell, at this point, I'm not sure our friendship is even worth saving.

"Liam."

She says my name so softly I barely hear it over the roar of the engine. I don't look at her.

"I'm sorry."

Her words pierce me. This is why I don't get romantically involved, why I hold a part of myself back from everyone, including Aislinn and Diana and even Ari. Ten-year-old me would have been ecstatic to learn I had an older brother, a mother who had loved me before I was born, who no doubt would have loved me if she hadn't passed away in the hospital shortly after I was born.

But the man I am now, the man forged by years of anger and grief and rejection in foster care, keeps his walls up. When you feel too deeply, you give people power.

I finally look at Aislinn. Remember that moment I found my parents kissing under the mistletoe, the moment I felt like everything was good and right in the world. A high that made the fall ten times more painful when I was left alone. I don't regret loving them for one second. But I'm smart enough to not open myself up to that kind of pain again.

CHAPTER TEN

Liam

KACEY AND THE other attendant thankfully arrive with dinner. They set down two plates and two water glasses on the long, sleek table close to the back of the cabin, followed a moment later by a third attendant with a bottle of wine and wineglasses.

Aislinn joins me at the table, her eyes downcast and her face wan. She barely touches the burrata salad with tomatoes, the filet mignon with roasted carrots and béarnaise sauce, or the pistachio mousse. The glass of wine remains full.

My anger slowly ebbs as she moves a slice of carrot around her plate with her fork. "I'm sure the attendants could find something else."

"No. Thank you. It looks delicious. I'm just not hungry."

Each word sounds like it's been being dragged out of her. I want to tell her to eat. I want to shout at her for ever thinking I could be anything like Dexter. I want her to trust me again.

I pause with my fork halfway to my mouth. Is that part

of why this is eating at me so much? Am I hurt more by her comment or by her distance?

You failed to keep her safe before. You could fail again.

Irritated with my subconscious, I set my fork down. But before I can say something, Aislinn's phone rings. She gets up and goes back to her seat, grimacing as she glances at the screen.

"Stephanie. She probably heard about us getting married."

Surprised, I lean back in my chair. "You didn't tell her about the ceremony?"

"No." Aislinn waits until it stops ringing before she speaks again. "We haven't been close for some time."

Part of what has made me good at my career is my ability to pick up on subtle tells, intonations, to read people. Beneath Aislinn's casual dismissal of her adoptive mother, there's a deep vein of pain.

"I'm sorry."

Aislinn nods slowly. "Thank you." She finally picks up her spoon and dips it into the mousse. My eyes follow the spoon, my body growing hard as her lips close around it, and she lets out a small sigh of contentment.

Thank God I'm sitting down. Walking would be a challenge.

I have to get a grip. Have to stop thinking about Aislinn this way. It's never going to happen.

Can't happen, I firmly remind myself.

"It was nice to meet Ari."

I breathe out. A neutral topic. "I'm glad."

"You two could be twins."

One corner of my mouth tilts into a half grin. "I've told him more than once I'm the more handsome of us two."

Aislinn smiles slightly. "I'm glad you're getting to know him."

My grin fades. I've been trying the past few months. After my fake engagement to Diana ended and she took a job for my brother, I was worried about her. I knew she was hiding something from me. So when an opportunity to meet with a client in Iceland popped up, I'd seized it, using the trip for both business and to check up on my friend. Finding out she'd slept with my half brother before learning of his relationship had been a shock. Discovering that she and Ari truly loved each other had been another twist I hadn't seen coming.

I'd told Ari on that trip I wanted to get to know him more. And I meant it. But it quickly proved to be much harder than I had anticipated. Listening to his stories about my birth mother—our mother—and imagining a life that could have been if she'd survived giving birth to me... That was a guilt I hadn't expected, knowing she gave her life and left behind a son to be raised by a coldhearted tyrant.

And if she had survived, I never would have met my adoptive parents, a fate I couldn't even begin to fathom.

The pain and the guilt had been too much. So I'd pulled back. Ari hadn't pushed, which deepened the guilt even more. Inviting him to the wedding had been a massive step, one I'd forced myself to make for Ari and Diana.

I pick up my wineglass. "I'm trying."

Aislinn tilts her head to one side, her eyes thoughtful.

Worried she's going to try and delve into my feelings, I ask, "Did you ever hear back from the DNA test?"

She freezes, her fingers tightening around her spoon. Slowly, deliberately, she lays it down on the table and leans back in her chair.

Aislinn used to say she could feel Diana's and my emotions like they were her own, a concept I struggled to understand. But I understand it now. I can feel the pain in the way her fingers grip the arms of the chair, the grief shining in her eyes, the anger in the tightness of her lips.

"Aislinn," I say quietly. "You don't have to tell me—"

"For so many years I dreamed about her." Her voice is so quiet I can barely hear it over the hum of the plane engines. "I thought she might have chosen foster care over a violent household, over not having enough money or an unsupportive family of their own. Maybe someone who had had that choice made for them while they pieced their life back together."

I wait as she pauses, picks up her wineglass and stares down into it with a blank gaze. Rallying herself for whatever.

"I got the DNA results back shortly after Dexter…after we started dating."

I note the pause, barely force myself to not pursue it.

"I found my birth mother on social media, had seen the pictures of her with a husband and two teenagers. Pictures of them in front of a little house in some suburban neighborhood, playing on a beach, going to one of the kids' baseball games." Her voice catches. "It hurt. It hurt so much. But I'd comforted myself with the hope that maybe she'd been searching for me all these years."

I stand and circle around the table, crouch next to her and grab her free hand with mine. She grips my fingers tightly with a strength that surprises me.

"I messaged her. She messaged me back, said she was glad I'd done well for myself and had found loving adoptive parents. She had moved on with her life and didn't want to dig into the past. Not when it could potentially hurt her husband and her children."

Rage swells inside me. Of all the people in this world who deserved a happily-ever-after, it was Aislinn. For her to experience the cruelest possible outcome, especially after all she'd been through, was unfathomable.

"Her children," Aislinn repeated softly. "A term that didn't include me."

I pluck the wineglass out of her hand, set it down on the table and pull her to her feet. I wrap my arms around her and hold her tight, one hand cupping the back of her head as I rock her.

She stays stiff in my arms for a long moment. Then she shudders, as if holding in the grief is too much, and slowly wraps her arms around my waist.

I don't know how long we stand there. But I don't let go until she gently pats me on the back and steps away. "Thank you."

She sinks down into her chair as I circle back to mine. Her eyes are red, but there are no tears. "Unfortunate, but she made her choice."

"A cruel, selfish woman."

Aislinn shrugs. "I don't know enough about why she made the choice to judge her. I'm just…sad."

"You give people too much credit."

"I used to." The lack of emotion in her voice sets off warning bells. "But I don't anymore. Logically, there are any number of reasons for her to have made her choices back then and her choices now. A touch of sadness is understandable. But to give in to anger or grief would be stupid."

I grit my teeth as I try to tamp down my own anger

and find the right words. "Trying to suppress your emotions isn't healthy, either."

Aislinn arches one dark golden brow. "Are you the pot or the kettle?"

Impressed and completely aware of the double standard I live by, I incline my head.

Before I can say anything else, her phone beeps again. She glances at it, then rolls her eyes. "Our wedding is already hitting the news." She sends me a small smirk. "More good PR."

I nod, even though acknowledging it makes me feel like dirt.

"What other campaigns do you have lined up? For your investment firm?" she asks as she reads the article on her screen.

I rattle off the list that my head of publicity came up with, including high-quality videos, client testimonials and press releases with some of the top publications in New York.

"Hmm."

I arch a brow at Aislinn's noncommittal sound. "Hmm?"

"It sounds good."

"But not great."

She shrugs one shoulder. "I think you should start a blog."

I stare at her. "A blog?"

"Yes. Topics that would appeal to your top-tier clients, of course, but articles that could be helpful to anyone. Building generational wealth, estate planning, investment diversification."

I blink. I've never been big on social media and having an online presence. But it's not a bad idea.

Aislinn looks up from her phone. It's a good idea. But it's the tiniest flare of interest in her eyes that has me nodding.

"I like it."

"I could write something up for you."

I smile at her. "I'd like that."

The smile she gives me, bright and hopeful, is worth writing a hundred blog posts. She glances back down at her phone. A moment later her body goes rigid. "Bill."

"Bill?"

Slowly, her head comes up. Her face is stricken, her eyes full of pain. "William Luther."

"Yes?"

She lets out a soft moan. "God, I'm an idiot."

I lean forward. "Perhaps I'm missing something."

"It was never about giving me a 'secret garden.' It was about putting on a show for your client and making sure he had a front-row seat." She holds up her phone.

The photos from our wedding are splashed all over a tabloid article, with a title touting the "elopement of the century" in a private greenhouse owned by billionaire William Luther.

Trepidation whispers across the back of my neck. Of course she would have to find this out right after reliving one of the worst moments of her life.

"Having Luther there was a benefit, yes." I reach for her hand, but she snatches it back. The small rejection is a kick to the gut. "I wanted to surprise you, too, Aislinn. To thank you."

She shakes her head. "Just stop. Stop, okay? I would have been fine with a courthouse wedding, Liam. I don't need all this pretense."

"No, but the public does." Damn it, I regret the words as soon as they're out of my mouth.

She closes her eyes and pinches the bridge of her nose. "Yes. The public." She lets out another long, harsh breath. "I apologize. You were just following our agreement—"

I stand. "Forget the agreement, Aislinn." I stalk around the table and stop in front of her, wait until she finally looks up at me. "Yes, I had the photographer leak the photos to someone in the press I knew would spread them quickly. And yes, Luther being there was a bonus. But he's the one who offered to marry us. My initial plan included an officiant, Diana, Ari, you and me."

"And the photographer," she adds quietly.

"Yes, and the photographer." I run a hand through my hair. "Damn it, Aislinn, that's part of why we're doing this."

"I know. I just…" She closes her eyes. I stare down at her, at the dark sweep of lashes against her cheeks, the full lips pressed so tightly together as she fights her demons alone. Again. When she finally opens her eyes, her walls are back in place. She's as cold and remote as she was the night I found her in the alcove at the gala. "I'll be all right."

"Don't do this."

"A few minutes ago, you had nothing to say to me."

"Yeah, while now I do have something to say." I reach out and grab her hand, tug her closer. "Don't push me away."

She braces her other hand on my chest.

The heat of her palm sears my skin through my shirt. The sudden, instant arousal nearly has me backing down. But I'm not giving up. Not now. I have to fight through it, focus on what's important.

Aislinn narrows her eyes at me. "I'm not pushing you away."

"Liar."

Temper flares in the emerald depths. I'm probably going to hell for finding it satisfying and oddly arousing. "I am not."

"Yes you are." I lean down. "You forget, I can read you like a book. Just how many secrets are you hiding, Aislinn?"

She stands her ground, her chin tilted up and her eyes fierce. As we stare each other down, awareness slams into me with the force of a freight train. My chest rises and falls as our breaths mingle. She shifts. Her breasts brush against my chest. The sound of her sharp inhale makes time stand still.

My eyes drop down to her mouth. How did I never notice how perfectly shaped it was before? Full, ripe lips. Soft and yielding when I kissed her just a few hours ago.

I need to kiss her again.

Just one more taste.

The first time I kissed her, I told myself it would be quick, passionless.

This time, I know better.

She meets me halfway as I crush my mouth to hers. The first time she was hesitant, testing. Now, she's on fire. She sinks into me, her arms circling around my neck as she kisses me back with a passion that rocks me to my foundation. I band one arm around her waist as my other hand sinks into her hair. Cool silk against the fire raging out of control under my skin.

I told myself one taste. But I can't walk away from this. Not yet.

I tease the seam of her lips with my tongue. Her mouth

parts on a gasp, and I take the kiss deeper, drink in every scent, every touch. Her hands move up my neck, her fingers diving into my hair. The slight tug makes me growl as my entire body goes hard. I press my hips against hers, shudder as she presses back against my cock.

There's a bedroom at the back of the plane. We have hours until we land. Hours for me to strip her naked and explore every inch of her body. Drive myself inside her and claim—

Stop. NOW.

I wrench myself away.

Aislinn stumbles back a few steps, swollen lips parted and her breath coming in short, rapid gasps. Just like mine as I fight to get myself back under control. Her eyes are wide, still bright with desire.

As I stare at her, try to grasp onto the threads of my sanity, a chill creeps into my chest. I'm not seeing Aislinn as my friend. I'm seeing her as a woman. A woman I want more than I've wanted anyone else in my life.

What the hell did I just do?

"Aislinn, I'm sor—"

"Stop." She raises a hand to her lips. Guilt punches through me as she touches her mouth with trembling fingertips, then looks away. "Just… I need to be alone."

I want to reach out, stop her. Apologize and figure out a way we can put this behind us. Go back to the way things were.

But as I watch her disappear into the bedroom at the back of the plane and close the door, feel the loss of her yet again, I know things will never be the same.

CHAPTER ELEVEN

Aislinn

THE BALLERINA SNAPS her fan shut and taps it on the shoulder of the male dancer in front of her. Basilio, I remember, the handsome barber. And the ballerina, Kitri, who has fallen for him instead of the wealthy man her father has picked out for him.

I've never been to a ballet before. I took dance classes when my favorite foster mother signed me up to attend with her daughter. I loved it; the leotards with the filmy skirts, learning the different positions, the routines set to relaxing classical music.

But this is different. As Basilio sweeps Kitri into his arms and draws within a breath of kissing her, my breath hitches. I recognize some of the movements. But everything else is so much more than I ever imagined a ballet to be. I've smiled a few times as Don Quixote and his bumbling but well-meaning lackey Sancho Panza stumble about. I've watched with wide eyes as the entire cast danced in unison.

And now, as Kitri caresses Basilio's face and he lifts

her up in front of a red sky with a lone windmill in the background, I'm mesmerized by their love story.

Liam shifts in the seat next to me. I probably look like a child leaning forward to see everything from our private box on the left side of the theater. But it's not just so I can see everything happening on stage. It's also so I can keep as much distance between Liam and myself as possible.

We arrived in Reykjavik yesterday. A private limo took us to a hotel overlooking the Old Harbor, not far from his brother Ari's geothermal energy company head-quarters. We barely said two words to each other on the drive. Thankfully Liam had reserved a two-bedroom suite for us. I'd taken the coward's way out and slipped into my room seconds after the concierge closed the door be-hind us.

I'd managed to make it to the bed before I let my tears fall. I buried my face in the pillow so Liam couldn't hear me cry. Those moments after the kiss on the plane had been like taking a knife to the chest, one he twisted when he'd started to apologize. I jumped between loving him and loathing him as tears ran down my face. Loving him for giving me a wedding he thought I would enjoy. Loath-ing him for turning it into a PR ploy. Loving him for com-ing after me, for not letting me hide. Loathing him for changing his mind and pushing me away.

I didn't just cry for him. I cried for the last year of my life, for my lost innocence and the fool I'd been. I'd cried for the months of lost friendship with Diana, especially the last four. Four months I can never get back because of my own pride and poor choices.

It was easier to focus on Diana, on my lost relation-ship with Eric and Stephanie, on how much my life had changed, than to think about Liam. To remember how being held by him, kissed by him, *wanted* by him, surpassed any dream I'd ever had.

Just a few seconds. But I know no man will ever make me feel as alive as Liam did.

Liam had left me alone until dinner. It had given me time to write up some more on my blog proposal, as well as a couple more ideas with sponsoring charity events and collaborating with financial journalists. It had given us something to talk about during dinner at a restaurant on the water. The venue had been stunning, with candlelit tables and chairs draped in faux fur blankets. Each dish had been a work of art, from a snow crab salad dressed with fennel greens to grilled sole surrounded by a ring of clams and dressed with a side of pickled plums.

I'd tried to focus on that instead of my husband. A challenge when I knew we had to at least look like we were enjoying ourselves. I saw more than one cell phone raised to capture a "discreet" photo. The only thing that had made conversing with Liam on a blog publication strategy bearable was the tension etched into the lines about his mouth. Knowing he was just as miserable as I was made it easier.

We had barely made it back inside our suite when alerts started popping up on my phone.

Lovebirds in Reykjavik!

Cinderella love story continues in Iceland.

Trouble in paradise? Exclusive insider says honeymooners barely speaking.

The last headline had been accompanied by a picture

of me looking decidedly glum as I stared off to the side. Liam looked equally miserable, his mouth set into a grim line, his hands folded on the table.

I wanted it to just be over. But I showed Liam the headline before I went to bed.

"Tomorrow," he said quietly, "we'll have to do better."

And then he turned and went inside his room, closing the door behind him. The click had been loud in the quiet stillness of the suite.

Down on the stage, the lovers dance off as Don Quixote lumbers onto the stage in his clunky armor. I smile slightly as children dance onto a miniature stage and re-enact the events of the first act.

"I'm impressed."

Liam's quiet murmur in my ear, coupled with his warm breath on my skin, makes me start.

"Oh?" I whisper back.

"The children dance better than Don What's-His-Name."

I bite my bottom lap to keep from laughing. "They're supposed to."

"Hmm."

I smile over my shoulder at him. He gives me a small grin back. For a moment our bond clicks into place, years of friendship arcing between us.

Liam's eyes drift down to my mouth. I breathe in sharply. His eyes dart back up to mine, and then he looks away. The bond snaps like it never existed.

I slowly turn back to the stage and sit up. I watch the rest of the second act like I'm seeing everything through a hazy mirror. I try to focus on the music, the dancers, the scenery. But it's hard.

It's so hard when the man I've loved for so long, the

man who kissed me like he'd die if he didn't, has treated me with cold indifference ever since. I walked away, yes. But I needed time to collect myself, to sort through what had happened. I also couldn't bear to hear him apologize, not when it had just replaced our wedding kiss as the best kiss of my life. Not when I felt, just for a moment, that maybe something could be possible between us.

Yet I should really be thanking Liam. I had just promised myself hours before our plane ride that I wouldn't allow myself to entertain any thoughts of our marriage turning into something more. That kiss had lured me toward that very thought. His almost-apology and subsequent silent treatment had plunged me back into cold reality.

The curtain falls down, marking the end of the second act. The lights come on, illuminating the vivid red birch walls of the concert hall.

Liam stands and turns to me with a smile. "Shall we?"

I force a small smile and take the offered hand.

Liam guides me through the throng of people outside our door to an elevator that whisks us up. My breath catches for an entirely different reason as we walk out onto the eighth floor.

The wall, a collection of geometric glass shapes that remind me of a beehive, looks out onto the Old Harbor. The sun set hours ago, but I can still make out the distant outline of a mountain on the other side of the water. Reykjavik hugs the shore, a collection of tall, slim buildings that slope down as the city spreads farther north.

"Beautiful, isn't it?"

I turn as Liam hands me a flute of champagne. He puts a hand at my back and guides me toward a tall table. I try to ignore the heat of his fingers through the fabric of my dress. And fail miserably.

"Yes, it is," I say before I take a generous gulp of my champagne.

"A little more refined than our high school theater."

I chuckle. Our school theater was a disaster; threadbare seats, a stage that groaned at inopportune times and curtains that always smelled of mothballs. But it also played host to one of my happiest memories; meeting Liam and Diana. "Hard to believe it's been twelve years."

"Twelve years this month."

Surprised, I glance at Liam. "You remember?"

He frowns. "Of course I remember."

A thought pokes me, a memory I can't quite grasp. And then it appears suddenly and with complete clarity.

"I stay in touch with Mrs. Scout, our old counselor," I mention casually.

Liam tenses beside me. "Oh? How is she?"

"She retired last year."

"Imagine that," he murmurs.

"And she received a check from a foundation for five hundred thousand dollars for 'exceptional service.'" I watch him like a hawk, note the slight tap of his fingers on the tabletop. "Know anything about that?"

"Good for her."

Warmth fills my chest as I gaze at Liam. I don't know why he holds everything so tightly, why he keeps us at a distance. But I know, no matter the challenges we're struggling with right now, that he's a good man.

Which makes my current predicament ten times harder. Each layer I peel back, each new detail I learn about him, the more I struggle to stay away from the edge of loving him.

Loving a man who will never share the same goals and dreams I do.

I swirl my champagne in my glass, watch the bubbles dance. "Why did you decide here for our honeymoon?"

I barely catch the hesitation in Liam's answer. "Unique. Beautiful. A chance to see Ari and Diana at the end."

I bite back a sigh. More secrets. Always more secrets.

The glass is nearly to my lips when Liam quietly says, "I wanted to see the country I may have grown up in."

I lower my glass and face him. "That makes sense."

He huffs a small, frustrated laugh. "Does it? Seems maudlin and unnecessary."

"But you're here," I say gently. "I'd give anything to know more about my heritage."

He looks at me then, his blue eyes surprisingly kind and warm. "A good point. Just…" He smiles slightly. "I'm not one to share."

"I know."

I don't mean to say the words out loud. But nonetheless they hit with accuracy as Liam's eyes darken. I look back out over the harbor.

An awkward thirty seconds of silence passes before Liam speaks. "Do you like the ballet so far?"

I nod as I watch a small boat, maybe a fishing boat, navigate across the harbor, its faint lights tiny against the dark expanse of water and sky. "It's a little sad, though."

Liam frowns. "What is?"

"Don Quixote is living in a fantasy world. No one's telling him the truth."

More silence. I mentally kick myself. After what I shared with Liam on the plane, I need to do a better job keeping my mouth shut. I can't confide in him the way I used to.

"He's happy, though," Liam says quietly. "Isn't that enough?"

I sigh. "I used to think so."

Liam moves closer until we're arm to arm. I keep my eyes focused on the boat, on its trek through the darkness, and off of my husband.

Unfortunately, I don't have to be looking at Liam to know he's there. To feel the warmth of his body through the sleeve of his suit, to hear the softness of his breathing and smell the rich cedar of his cologne.

"What would make you happy, Aislinn?"

I almost don't answer. But then I realize this is an opportunity. To once again remind myself of the boundaries I must keep. Liam is attracted to me, yes, something that once would have made me ecstatic. Now it's just painful. I'm under no illusions that that attraction will turn into love. And even if it did, there's no future for us.

I look up at him, meet his pale blue gaze head-on. "A family of my own."

His eyes widen slightly. Understanding, empathy and a hint of fear that tells me, perhaps even more than Liam could ever say himself, that we will never be. "Aislinn…"

"Not us, Liam." I smile slightly. "You've always been vocal about how you feel about being a parent. And I have no desire to marry again after we…" My voice fades, and I glance around to make sure no one is eavesdropping. "After we part ways."

"Adoption?"

This time my smile is real. "Yes. I want children. I want a home with kids running around, happy and well-fed, kids who know they're safe and loved and will never have to worry about not having a roof over their head again."

Something dark flits across Liam's face. "It sounds nice."

"What is it?"

He shakes his head. "It's nothing. I—"

"You asked me on the plane to not shut you out." I give in to the urge to reach out and gently squeeze his hand. "You still want me to share."

He stares at me, his eyes uncharacteristically bleak. "Aislinn…" His gaze shifts and locks onto something over my shoulder. The bleakness vanishes in an instant, replaced by a cold cunning that induces an involuntary shudder. "Phones. People trying to snap pictures of us."

Tension grips my shoulders. I start to turn, but Liam reaches out and cups my face in his hand. Heat washes over me as I meet his eyes.

"Focus on me." His thumb strokes along my cheekbone, igniting little sparks that turn into fires racing across my skin. "There's just us. No cameras, no nosy bastards."

The uncharacteristic profanity startles a laugh out of me. "Liar."

He smiles down at me. "But it made you laugh. I wish you'd laugh more like that. Like you used to."

He leans down, and I sway forward to meet him, my eyes drifting shut…only to fly open when he brushes his lips across my forehead.

Before I can sort through my racing thoughts, the lights flicker and a bell dings.

"Since we have a private box, we're allowed to take our champagne back in," Liam murmurs.

I nod, not trusting myself to speak.

He once again lays a hand at the base of my spine and steers me back to the elevator. Out of the corner of my eye I see a woman raise her phone in our direction.

I suck in a deep breath, then slip an arm around Liam's waist and lay my head on his shoulder. His body tenses beneath my touch.

He may not feel any of the emotions I do. But at least I have the satisfaction of knowing he's just as physically unsettled as me.

Cold, hollow satisfaction.

Liam

The elevator doors whoosh shut. I spend the next seven seconds focusing on the descending numbers and keeping my eyes off my wife.

My wife, who is the definition of a siren tonight, dressed in a scarlet sheath dress that clings to every curve I never paid attention to. She chose another off-the-shoulder design that reminds me of her wedding dress. Never in my life have I thought a woman's shoulders to be sexy. But now, as the doors snick open, and she walks out ahead of me, I entertain graphic images of kissing along her ridges, the curve of her arm, scraping my teeth along her skin.

It's not just the physical I find sexy. It's the whole woman: strong, powerful, determined to rise above the parade of heartbreaks she's suffered.

As we move into our private box, I'm aware of more than one man eyeing her appreciatively. With my ring sparkling on her finger and her hair falling in a smooth, golden waterfall to her shoulders, she's beautiful.

I wait for her to sit before taking my own seat. Then, with a nasty thought for the men lusting after my wife,

I slide my arm around her shoulders. She stiffens but doesn't pull away.

The lights dim. The curtain rises on the third act. Slowly, Aislinn relaxes. Despite her best intentions to remain aloof, the ballet pulls her back in. The tightness about her mouth eases as her lips curve up.

It's not hard to picture her as a mother. Reading her favorite books to them at bedtime, cheering them on at a game or wiping away their tears.

My heart twists in my chest. But this time, instead of the bone-deep certainty that kids are not a part of my future, there's a flicker of something else. Something I've never experienced before.

Longing.

I squelch it before it can take root. Having children is something I crossed off my list after a few years in foster care. I can barely summon enough emotion for my friends, let alone my long-lost brother. There's no way I'd be emotionally capable as a father. And given how many kids I lived with who had been abandoned by cold, detached parents, I'm not risking passing that trauma onto another child.

Even if I've occasionally wondered what it would be like to be a dad, all I have to remember is the words of the last foster father I ever had before I was moved into the group home.

I hope you never have kids.

I'd already decided I didn't want a family. Much as I loathed my final foster family, the words cemented my choice. I wasn't cut out to be a dad. Never will be. But things I can control—my career, the wealth of my clients— those are goals I can pursue. Milestones I can achieve without worrying who I'm hurting or who I might lose.

It also gives me vicious satisfaction every time I think of the words uttered during my time in foster care. I heard more than one foster parent murmur to their spouse or a social worker that they'd be surprised if I amounted to anything after graduation. Now, I'm wealthier than any of them will ever be. I have the stability they never offered me.

I glance at Aislinn out of the corner of my eye. Even if I sometimes wonder what life would be like with someone in it, I've made the right choices.

The third act continues. I try to pay attention to the dancers, the elaborate sets, the orchestra. But it's hard to focus when the realization that Aislinn and I will never be compatible pulses through me, a certainty that shouldn't matter.

But it does.

At last the curtain falls. The cast comes out for several curtain calls. Aislinn stands and applauds, a slight smile on her face.

I hold out my arm as she turns to me. "Ready?"

She nods and takes my arm without looking at me. I catch more than one curious glance directed our way as we make our way to the coat check.

I lean down to whisper in her ear. "Who would I be best as? Don Quixote or Sancho Panza?"

The question works. Her full lips, colored the same red as her dress, slide up into a smile. "You could look good in armor. But somehow I think Gamache is more your style."

I arch a brow. "The rich, spoiled nobleman?"

She reaches up and flicks her finger against my hair. "You'd look good in a tri-corner with a feather."

A flash interrupts our teasing.

Aislinn's face falls a moment before she smooths out her expression into a bland mask. "Well done."

"Ash—"

She shakes her head slightly even as she keeps the fake smile pasted on her face. "It's fine, Liam. I'm tired and on edge. It'll be okay."

Just a couple hours ago I was apprehensive about spending time together in the villa Ari recommended in northern Iceland. There will be no fancy restaurants, no operas or other opportunities for photographers to keep us under their microscope. Just Aislinn, me and miles of endless snow and ice.

Right now, as I feel her pull away even while she presses her body closer to mine, I want that time with her. Want a chance for us to hit Reset after the months of being apart, after my stupid decision to kiss her on the plane.

Want us to get back to where we were before Dexter entered her life and changed everything.

We step out into the winter air. I glance toward the dark outline of the mountain and the snow-drenched slopes. The first time I was in Iceland, my primary focus had been Diana and finding out why she had been so distant. I'd been aware of the fact that this was my homeland.

But now, with the picture of my mother tucked snugly in the pocket of my suit, I'm all too conscious of my heritage. The guilt is ever-present: guilt for what happened to my birth mother; guilt for wanting to know more about her after everything my adoptive parents gave me. It's a constant companion, one I haven't been able to shake ever since I laid eyes on her picture.

I surprised myself when I suggested Iceland to Aislinn. It had been the morning after I gave her the ring. I'd walked in to see her at the kitchen table, reading a book and stirring a spoon in a cup of hot tea. The urge to share Iceland with her, not just a whirlwind trip but a true visit to both the glittering city my brother called home and the northern shores where my birth mother was raised, came out of nowhere. But it was an urge I couldn't shake.

I don't know if I would have taken this step if I wouldn't have known she'd be by my side. I doubt I'll ever be able to express to Aislinn how much her being here with me means.

As I open the door of the limo for Aislinn, a cruel voice echoes in my head.

Not able? Or too afraid?

CHAPTER TWELVE

Aislinn

CHRISTMAS IN NEW YORK used to be my favorite part of winter. The bright lights, the huge Christmas tree and skating rink at Rockefeller Center, the snow-covered trees in Central Park.

It's nothing compared to Iceland.

The landscape passes by as Liam navigates the Jeep down the road. Snow-drenched land stretches out on either side of the road before sweeping up into soaring hills. Farmhouses and trees dance in and out view through the swirling snow.

I burrow deeper into my coat. The Jeep is warm, my seat heater on full blast. But the temperature between Liam and me rivals the frigid weather outside.

"I posted my first blog post."

Surprised, I glance over at Liam. "Oh?"

"Just on LinkedIn. It's a start."

I pull out my phone. There's just enough of a signal for me to pull up his profile and the link. "'Securing Your Family's Future,'" I read out loud. "'Build and Protect Generational Wealth.'"

"Lengthy and a touch austere," he replies.

"I like it, though." I scroll through the article. It's well-written, with a touch of humor that makes me smile even as it makes me think about things I could be doing to prepare for the family I hope to have one day. "I like it a lot."

"Thank you."

The sincerity in his voice has me glancing over. But Liam is staring straight ahead, his eyes fixed on the horizon.

I stifle a sigh and lean my head against the glass of the window.

The three days in Reykjavik flew by. I spent most of the days following the ballet wandering the streets and ducking into various shops. We went out a couple of times to sell the story of a couple in love on their honeymoon and managed to make stilted conversation. But aside from those brief moments in public, we barely saw each other. Even on the flight from Reykjavik's airport to the regional airport in Akureyri in northern Iceland, we barely spoke.

I saw a few pictures of the villa. Four bedrooms, glass walls and stunning views of the mountains and the deep blue waters of a fjord. Plenty of places for me to spend the next week taking what joy I can out of this honeymoon and staying as far away from my husband as possible.

At least in Reykjavik, I could wander. But that came with the price of paparazzi following everywhere I went. Sometimes they were brazen. Sometimes they were sneaky. Pictures appeared online within an hour of us returning to our hotel room every time, and sometimes even a few photos of just me. Each one made me feel like a liar, even as it reminded me of the reason why I'm here.

But here in the northern part of the country, I'm going to be stranded with Liam out in the middle of a frozen wilderness. I'd almost rather deal with the paparazzi. I'm surprised Liam picked a spot so far away when the goal of this honeymoon was to sell our romance.

I hear the clicking of the blinker and glance over. "Are we stopping?"

"Yes." Liam's face has turned unusually tense, his fingers tight on the wheel.

Confused, I look forward and see a sign. "Goðafoss Waterfall," I murmur.

"Waterfall of the Gods," Liam replies as he steers into a parking lot and puts the Jeep in Park. "It's nearly a fifty-minute walk to the waterfall."

My eyebrows shoot up. "Okay."

He stares straightforward out the windshield. "You can stay here."

I bristle but bite back my initial retort. Something else is going on. "Do you want me to stay here?" I ask.

He taps his finger against the steering wheel. Once. Twice. Then, finally, "It would be nice to have you there."

The admission costs him. Whatever is going on, it's enough for us to put aside our differences.

"All right."

We take a few minutes to get bundled in our winter gear and then set out along the path. The wind is fierce, but the winter pants, coat and face covering are relatively cozy as we walk along the snow-dusted path. A rope lines most of the way, tracing a trail through craggy rocks, up and down hills.

"A lava field," Liam finally says when he catches me crouching down to look at one of the formations. "Thousands of years old."

Amazed, I barely stop myself from touching it. "And

here I thought that some of the oldest places in New York were incredible for being hundreds of years old."

The rest of the walk is silent. Yet, unlike the silence since our unfortunate kiss, this one is companionable. By unspoken agreement, we've decided to put aside our differences for the moment. I want to ask questions, but I don't have the right. Whatever demons Liam is facing are his to battle. And, as I've learned from past experience, he'll most likely keep them to himself.

The onset of sound is so gradual it doesn't register at first—a shushing that grows into a dull roar. We crest a hill, and my jaw drops.

"Wow."

Torrents of water tumble over the lip of a cliff, forming several falls that descend to a large pool. Curtains of ice drape over the edge and have formed clumps in the pool—winter trying to make its mark despite the river's persistence. It's like something out of a dream.

I look at Liam. He's pulled his balaclava down so that I can see most of his face—the tightness of his jaw, lips pressed together.

Slowly, I reach out and lay a hand on his shoulder. "Liam?"

Wordlessly, he reaches up, unzips a pocket over his chest and pulls out a clear bag with a photograph in it.

I take it. My heart drops.

It's an older photo, slightly faded at the edges and creased in a few places. But the image is still clear: Goða-foss in summer, the lava rocks dotted with green, and the water sparkling clear as it tumbles over the basin.

And there, just on the edge of the photograph, is a young woman with dark hair, pale blue eyes and a round belly.

I turn the photo over.

Mamma og ungbarn.

Liam translates softly. "Mama and baby."

"Your mother." I flip the photo back over and stare at the smiling woman who, just months later, would lose her life.

"The photo was taken a few months before I was born. Ari and our mother used to take long drives, weekend trips, whenever Ari's father was home. This was the last place they came before she had me."

I trace a finger over her face—the sweet smile, the eyes so like Liam's.

"She loved you," I say.

The words slip out. I mentally curse, but before I can say anything else, Liam looks down at the photo.

"She did."

We stand there together, staring down at the photo, listening to the roar of the falls.

A million thoughts run through my head, a thousand possibilities of what I could say. But none of it seems right. Liam has lost not only one mother, but two. What does one say to that? Especially to a man who keeps himself bottled up so tightly?

I breathe out as my eyes roam over the stark, wintry landscape. Liam has hurt me, yes. But he's also been there for me more times than I can count over the years. Him sharing something so deeply personal is a gift I can recognize through my own pain.

So I stand and wait.

Liam

My mother smiles up at me from the picture in Aislinn's hand. I never met her, yet she feels so familiar that I can almost imagine her voice, hear her laugh as the photograph was taken.

Aislinn glances up at me. There are no empty platitudes, no mumbled words of apology or false statements of hope. That's something I've always appreciated about her. Even though she always maintained such a sunny outlook on life, I never once heard her say something just for the sake of saying it. She always knew when to listen, when to give space and when to give support. That, at least, hasn't changed. And God, I'm grateful for it.

The last few days have been torture. One minute I'm furious with myself for kissing her, for wanting her as badly as I do. The next I'm angry with her for once again being able to withdraw so easily, to go out to the ballet and dinner and act like everything's fine even as I'm burning on the inside.

"I don't know what to feel."

I feel like I'm wrenching the words from some deep pit buried in my chest. I don't share. But right now, it feels like the right thing to do. The last year may have been different, but the eleven years prior to that, Aislinn has always been there. Small gestures I once took for granted until suddenly they were no longer there.

"Understandable."

I hold my hand out. She lays the photo in my palm. I hold it up, positioning the picture so I can see exactly where my mother stood thirty-one years ago.

"Losing Mom and Dad…"

Grief tightens my chest. Most days I don't think about them. Don't think about the counselor pulling me out of class, the principal sitting next to me and awkwardly patting me on the shoulder as they told me my parents were dead. I stared at them. Screamed at them. Begged.

None of it changed the fact that my parents were gone.

"They never concealed my adoption from me. I wondered sometimes, but I was happy." I look at the picture once more before slipping the picture back into my pocket and zipping it up. "When they died, Child Services did a search for any living relatives. They didn't find anyone."

Aislinn shifts beside me. "A different kind of pain. The not knowing, wondering why."

"It made me angry. So angry I scared the first foster family I was placed with. I didn't last four weeks."

Aislinn's head whips around, and she stares at me, eyes wide. "I didn't know that."

"Not something most people respond well to." My jaw tightens. "They automatically think of you as the stereotypical foster kid. Don't get me wrong, I was an ass. I talked back to my foster dad and snapped at my foster mom. And then their son told me I needed to show them a little gratitude for taking in a runt."

"What?"

The outrage in Aislinn's voice makes my mouth quirk up. "I punched him."

"Good."

"Good except I got kicked out." I remember every moment of the walk from their porch to the car waiting to take me to my next home. Hot summer day, sun beating down on the back of my neck, mirroring the anger inside me. The anger covering a grief so large I didn't know to process it. So I concealed it. "It's been hard for me to connect with people since then."

"Again, understandable." Aislinn shakes her head. "The system is overworked. But it still failed you. You were ten years old, and you'd just lost both your adopted parents. Of course you were angry and grieving."

"Angry is one thing. Rage…" I breathe in deeply. "Rage is another beast."

My mind flashes back to another winter's day. The snow wasn't white and sparkling but gray and sludgy. Aislinn walking beside me talking a mile a minute as we headed to Diana's to walk the little puppy she'd sneaked into her backyard.

The cry had barely sounded before I was running. I knew the sounds—the whip of the belt, the frightened howls of the dog—knew what they meant. And when I barreled through the broken backyard gate of Diana's foster home, I wanted to kill the foster father who had beaten her.

I can still remember the fury, feel the murderous pulse in my veins as I'd punched the old drunk over and over again. His eyes had rolled back into his head as he fell to the ground. And still I hit him.

It had only been Aislinn screaming my name that broke through my focus, only her small hands clutching my arm and tugging me away that kept me from killing a man that day.

I curl my hands into fists at my sides. "I almost killed someone, Aislinn."

"Don't." She lays a hand on my arm, almost the exact same place she laid her hands twelve years ago. "You stopped, Liam. You made a choice that day. You saved two lives and possibly others."

"I wanted to hurt him."

"As did I." She rubs soothing circles on my bicep.

I can barely feel it through the thickness of my parka, but I'm so damned grateful for it. Grateful for the comfort she's offering, the understanding.

"If you need someone to forgive you, Liam, I do."

My throat constricts even as my chest lightens, re-
leased from a burden I hadn't realized I'd been carrying
all these years. I glance down at Aislinn, at this woman
who even after all she's been through can still see straight
to the heart of everything. A woman who has been a constant friend through all my ups and downs. One of the
few people to stay.

And I nearly screwed it all up by kissing her. I don't
know why, after years of friendship, I'm suddenly struggling with these feelings. But it has to stop. I almost lost
Aislinn once. I'm not going to lose her again just because
I can't keep myself under control. Aislinn may be telling
herself now that she never wants to get married again,
but she deserves more than casual sex. And that's all I
have to give.

I've been down the road of losing people I care about
one too many times. I don't think I'm capable of opening
my heart up to anyone again, and even if I were, I don't
want to. Standing here, feeling the grief clawing at me,
the memories from my past like a persistent knock at the
base of my skull, are reminders enough.

"Going through all of that changed me."

"Yeah, it would change anyone."

I breathe in deeply as I force out the next words. "What
I'm saying is it's one of the reasons why I don't do relationships."

She stares at me for a long second, then nods. "So this
isn't you finally sharing something from your past and
opening up to me?" she asks. "This is a warning?"

Irritated, I turn and face her. "I just shared one of the
most painful moments of my life with you. Explain to me
how that's not sharing."

"You shared, yes, and I appreciate that, Liam. You've

hardly shared any bit of yourself with Diana or me over the years."

The pain in her voice surprises me. "I told you, I'm not used to sharing."

"No, but you sure were content to let Diana and me share. Hell, you even encouraged it. And the one time when I think that you're finally opening up to me, you just turn it into a way to drive us apart even further." She shakes her head. "If you were wondering if our kiss was suddenly making me picture this marriage reaching its fourth anniversary or that I might be imagining a nursery for our kid, I know better. I know you, Liam. I know those things aren't in your future, and if you think that I would pressure you into something I know you don't want, then you don't know me, either."

She's walking back down the path before I can even respond.

I stand, staring at the spot where she stood just a few moments ago.

What the hell just happened?

Aislinn and I had always had the easiest friendship. I could be myself with her, relax, let my guard down. No, I wasn't into sharing bits and pieces of my past. But damn it, not sharing doesn't make me a bad friend.

Her accusation that I encouraged her and Diana to share lingers, though. Yes, there's some merit to it. I wanted to keep them safe. I wanted to be the friend, the brother they never had.

And you liked being their protector. Having something else to focus on.

I silence the ugly voice in my head and start back down the path, the waterfall continuing its incessant roar be-hind me.

CHAPTER THIRTEEN

Liam

ARI'S RECOMMENDATION DOESN'T DISAPPOINT. The villa, constructed of stone and glass, sits on top of a hill overlooking the narrow strip of sea below and the snowcapped mountains in the distance.

"Wow."

Aislinn walks from wall to wall, her eyes drinking in the sights. I smile slightly. She always sees things I don't. Diana notices details, too, but like me, she tends to focus on people, on reading their tells and signs so she can anticipate, prepare. Aislinn, by whatever miracle, simply saw the good. It used to worry me, made me think of her as a little sister to be protected from the truth of the world.

Definitely not a little sister anymore.

Blood rushes south. My cock starts to swell. I mentally swear, then leave Aislinn in the living room as I explore the rest of the villa.

All the rooms boast soaring ceilings and massive windows. The master bedroom is at the back of the house with its own private door onto one of several patios. This one, I remember as I note the steam rising from the far end of the patio, has stairs that lead down into a hot spring mineral pool.

I wander back out into the living room. "Do you have a preference on bedrooms?"

"No. Thank you," Aislinn adds, almost as an after-thought.

"The one toward the back has a private patio that opens onto a hot spring."

She quirks her head to the side. She's always done that when she's interested, a minute gesture most people probably miss. "That sounds nice."

"Then you take it."

She turns, her breath coming out in a heavy sigh as she crosses her arms. "We're stuck here for three days. I don't want to fight anymore."

"I don't, either."

"Okay. So we kissed. It happened. Now it's over."

I slide my hands into my pockets—clear, concise, emotionless. A dream response. So why the hell does it settle like an incessant itch between my shoulder blades? "Sounds good to me."

Aislinn nods. "We both had rough years. We've barely seen each other. Ours is a business arrangement, but the nature of it is rooted in ideas of romance and love."

She spits out the last few words with a derision that makes me ache for her, or rather the woman she used to be. I want nothing to do with love, but I wanted it for her. It's only understandable that we would get caught up.

I nod. "Yes. Understandable."

Aislinn lets out a deep breath. "So we're on the same page. No more kissing."

"There might still be occasions in the future when the situation warrants the kiss."

She rears back so drastically that I don't know whether to be amused or offended. "There are plenty of couples out there who don't kiss in public."

"Couples in love?"

"Yes."

"Like who?"

She blinks rapidly. "British royalty. Isn't it like against royal protocol or something?"

"As flattered as I am that I'm being compared to a prince, I think their situation is a little different than ours."

I step closer, intrigued when Aislinn takes a step back.

"We just agreed that we weren't going to talk about the kiss anymore." Color creeps up her neck—a soft, delicate rose that makes her skin glow.

"I'm not suggesting we kiss now, or anytime soon." Another step forward on my part. Another step back on hers. "I'm merely pointing out the possibility of it in the future."

She runs a hand through her hair, dislodging several strands that frame her face. I hope she grows it back long. I remember a night three years ago when she wore it loose—a political fundraiser. I asked her to dance, and as I spun her in a circle, she threw back her head and laughed, her hair falling down her back in a golden cascade.

I stop. Did I really think that? Back then?

"Can we talk about that later?" Aislinn's question yanks me back to the present.

"Of course." I glance around the massive living room. "Obviously no need for it here."

"Yes."

The doorbell rings.

"I'll get it." Aislinn darts forward like a frightened bunny. As she passes by me, that dark scent of rose lingers.

I walk over to the window and lean my head on the cold glass. It's bothering me—the realization that four years ago, I was noticing the way Aislinn's hair looked as we danced. Have I been wanting her all this time?

I should be disgusted. Instead, I'm thinking about how I want to sink my hands into her hair, feel the silk against my fingers.

"Catering delivery."

I turn around. Aislinn is standing on the far side of the living room, her arms crossed over her chest, her eyes wary.

"Sounds good. Are you hungry?"

She shakes her head.

"Then maybe I'll see you at dinner."

"Yeah. Okay." She starts to turn away, then stops. "The caterer said there's a snowstorm they're keeping an eye on, but they think it'll pass south of here."

I shrug. "Iceland is used to snow. I'm sure we'll be fine even if the storm does hit."

I watch her walk away. Force myself to let her. She's in the same house. She's not going to disappear anytime soon. And I need this time to figure out what the hell is going on with me.

For so many years, I've shut out most of my feelings. Loving Aislinn and Diana, accepting them as sisters, was the closest I got—a huge leap for me, but one that still provided some distance. I threw myself into the role of protector, partially because I wanted them to finally be safe, to have the lives they deserved.

But I can also admit that part of it was selfish. Protecting them, being their friend, gave me a purpose—something a little more personal than my goal of achieving my own wealth and independence, of never having to depend on anyone ever again.

Mercenary. Self-centered. Does it matter whether I've subconsciously noticed Aislinn before all of this? Even if I could let down my walls, I'm not the kind of man she deserves.

Which means no matter how much I want to kiss her, I can't. She's been through hell. I'm not going to drag her into mine.

My phone rings. "Whitlock."

"Mr. Whitlock? This is Bjarki, the manager of the villa." He sounds relieved. "Did you and your wife make it to the villa all right?"

"Yes, thank you."

"Good." Bjarki clears his throat. "I'm glad because I was just informed that the bridge leading off the highway to the villa collapsed."

"Excuse me?"

"Five minutes ago. A glacial outburst flood overwhelmed the bridge. The catering staff just made it across before the water came." His tone takes on an edge. "Foolish engineer used a timber pile foundation, and I warned him—"

"Is there another way out?" I interrupt.

"By helicopter, yes. Except..."

"Except what?" I ground out.

"High winds are forecast for the next several days. If it holds, the soonest I could get a helicopter to you would be early next week."

I stand there with the phone pressed to my ear, blood roaring in my ears. What are the odds that a split second after I decide to keep my distance from my wife, I'd be trapped with her in the middle of nowhere?

Aislinn

I throw back the covers and stand, grateful for the thick rug spread out across the floor. I grab a robe I tossed over a nearby chair and shrug into it before walking over to the window. There's nothing outside but snow, the white muted by the night as the storm howls around us.

This can't be good.

I drag a hand over my face. Three days. It was supposed to be three days in Iceland. If the wind keeps up like this, the helicopter won't be visiting anytime soon.

Another gust slams against the villa. I glance at the clock. Only one in the morning, but I'm not going back to sleep anytime soon. Not with the storm raging and my thoughts swirling in my head.

I quietly ease open my door and glance down the hall. Low lights along the baseboards create a warm, comforting glow. I pad softly down the hall.

Liam picked a bedroom on the opposite side of the house. Which is a good thing, I remind myself as I head toward the kitchen. The more distance between us, the better. Especially after he started talking about the potential of us having to kiss in the future.

My pulse went wild with the possibility of it. I don't need that right now. Can't deal with it. Especially when he made me feel like he was hunting me in the living room that first day, teasing the possibility of another kiss.

The man is so confusing. One minute, I think he's opening up to me emotionally and trying to reestablish our friendship. Then he reveals that he's reminding me that we can never be more than friends, right before he starts teasing me about us having to kiss again to sell our fake marriage. And now, since we learned about the bridge, he's been nothing but respectful, polite last night during dinner and cordial when he bid me goodnight before going to his room.

It's driving me crazy.

I walk into the kitchen and head for the fridge. I'm reaching for the handle when a voice speaks from the shadows.

"Good morning."

I shriek and spin around.

Liam is leaning casually against the counter with a steaming mug in his hands. And, damn it, he's only wearing pajama pants. Black silky pajama pants, the waistline clinging to his muscular hips, the silky material following the long line of his legs. One barefoot is crossed over the other at his ankle, and I have no idea why I find that sexy. But I know why I find his upper body sexy. Carved muscles dusted with a dark smattering of hair. Bulging biceps as he braces one hand on the counter behind him.

"Are you flexing?"

His smile is quick and white in the darkness of the kitchen. "Is that a pickup line?"

I roll my eyes, but I'm grateful for his humor. "What are you doing in here?"

"I could ask the same of you."

I glance toward the wall of glass at the far end of the kitchen. Still more white. Endless white. The storm.

"Guess the caterer was wrong."

I nod, my eyes focused on the swirling snow. "Do you think we'll be stuck here?"

I hear the tremor in my voice before I feel it in my chest—the tightening, the feeling of the world starting to press in on me. I try to keep my breathing even, try to fight it, but it's so hard.

"Aislinn." Liam's voice washes over me. I mentally respond to the sound of it, hold on to it like a lifeline. "Why are you in the kitchen?"

I breathe in deeply. "The storm. What else?"

I can't tear my eyes away from the snow, but I can sense him, can feel the heat of his body as he moves closer. The refrigerator hums. The furnace. Good. Two more. My heart beating. His footsteps on the floor.

"Close your eyes."

I follow his gentle command. My eyes drift shut.

"What do you smell?"

I inhale deeply, then release a cleansing breath. "Some kind of cleaner. Chocolate. Some kind of alcohol, like whiskey." I smile slightly. "My shampoo. And…" *You.* "Cedar."

"What else?"

My eyes fly open.

Liam is standing just a few inches away, his eyes burning into mine.

"Your cologne."

Liam's eyes drop down to my mouth. God, I want him to kiss me so badly. When he kissed me on our wedding day, it was unexpected and sensual. When he kissed me on the plane, he showed me a world I had never experienced. And now…now I can only imagine what our next kiss would be like.

I raise my face to his, start to lean forward, and then Liam steps back.

I jerk back like I've been slapped.

"Are you okay?" His words sound like rock scraping against rock—harsh, rough.

"Yes. I'm better." I glance back at the window. "It's just situations when I feel trapped, like there's no escape. Thank you."

He nods, then holds up his mug. "Drink?"

I swallow hard. Normal conversation. That's what I need. "Sure."

He walks over to the stove and pours what I realize is hot chocolate out of a kettle into another mug. I watch the ripple of muscles across his back as he moves about the kitchen. My fingers ache to reach out, follow the lines of his body. He turns back to me and sets the steaming mug on the counter, along with a bottle.

"I'll let you pick your poison."

I grab the bottle of brandy, uncap it and pour a very generous amount into my mug.

Liam's eyebrows shoot up. "Do I need to check on you later?"

"No." I hold up my mug in a toast to him. "Thanks for the drink. And the help. Good night."

I'm halfway across the kitchen when I hear him murmur my name. But I keep moving, walking out and back down the hall to my room.

CHAPTER FOURTEEN

Aislinn

I CLOSE THE door behind me and walk over to the bed, flicking on the switch that turns on the fireplace as I go. Flames crackle to life around the synthetic logs as I shrug off my robe and ease back under the covers.

Things will be different once we're back in New York. Once we both have things to distract us—Liam opening his firm, me figuring out what I want to do… I glance at my phone. Figuring out things like whether or not I want to accept the job offer I received this afternoon from the Foster Foundation. A month ago, they wanted nothing to do with me. And now they want to hire me without even conducting an interview.

My fingers tighten around the mug. I'm alone in my bedroom in northern Iceland in the middle of a snow-storm. I'm going to grant myself a couple of minutes to have a pity party. It seems like a cruel joke that I could be wanted by so many people, yet never for myself—only for what I can do for them. By Eric to elevate his campaign. By Dexter to use my political connections to both protect him and advance his agenda. By the Foster

Foundation, for my newfound notoriety as the heroine in a love story so outlandish people want to believe. And Liam. Once upon a time, Liam wanted to be friends with me simply because he liked me. But now...now that's all changed, too.

I take a sip of my drink. My eyes widen. Wow, I had a heavy hand with the brandy on that one. At least it's good brandy. Great, actually. Some of the best I've ever had. And beneath the strong vanilla and spice of the alcohol, I can taste the richness of some of the best hot chocolate I've ever had. The same scents I smelled as Liam helped me stabilize.

A pressure grows between my thighs. I shift my legs, sit up in bed, take another sip of my drink.

None of it helps. And now there's the tingling to deal with. Subtle threads of sensation traveling up through my belly, winding their way through my body until every nerve ending is pulsing.

This is ridiculous. I should not be having this kind of reaction simply because a man stood a few feet away from me. But I am, and aside from getting drunk, which will just leave me with a horrible headache in the morning, there's only way reasonable way to deal with this.

I set my mug on the nightstand and ease down into the pillows. I close my eyes and breathe in, then out. Slowly, my muscles relax despite the need now beating a demanding rhythm in my veins. I reach up, cup my breasts in my hands and moan as I remember how it felt to be pressed against Liam's chest. I pull my top down, lightly graze my bare nipples with my fingertips as I imagine his mouth closing over one, then the other.

I arch my hips up off the bed and ease my sleep shorts and panties off. I keep one hand on my breasts while I skim the other over my stomach, past my hips, and down to my core.

When my fingers brush my skin, I hesitate. My thighs are damp, my skin hot. Slowly, I explore my body, imagine that it's Liam's fingers, hands, mouth on me. I've never indulged in a daydream like this before.

And it's so damn good.

The pressure builds. Presses against me. I'm climbing up, moaning, saying his name as I imagine him grabbing my hips and—

My door opens. Mortification roots me in place as Liam and I make eye contact.

This can't be happening. This is a dream. A nightmare. I'm going to wake up anytime…

Except one hand is still pressed between my thighs. The other is still cupped around my breast. I'm naked except for the tank top shoved down below my breasts.

I start to sit up, to reach for the blanket at the bottom of the bed as I fight against the sheer humiliation of being caught in such a vulnerable position. Did he hear me say his name? Will he even want to continue the marriage after this?

"Don't stop."

I freeze. Then, slowly, I turn my head to stare at him. Liam is still standing in the doorway, hands fisted by his sides, his bare chest rising and falling as he devours me with his gaze.

Bad idea. Very, very, very bad idea.

Slowly, I lean back into the pillows. The humiliation lingers, adding an edge of discomfort. But the fire in Liam's eyes, seeing the tension in every taut line of muscle, the way his fingers are curling, then uncurling, gives me a sense of power. Pure feminine satisfaction.

Liam wants me. I want him. If this is as close as we're going to get, so be it.

I slide my hand back between my legs. This time I tease, taunt myself and him as I glide my fingers up and down my thighs. The slight scratch of my fingernails, the softer touch of my fingertips, has my breath catching and my back arching.

I glance over at Liam. Then moan when I see him ease the waistband of his pants down and grip his cock with one hand.

His very large cock.

We stare at each other as he strokes himself. My hand moves to my core. I slide a finger inside myself, my hips bowing off the bed as I imagine Liam between my legs. He strokes faster, his breathing intensifying as his eyes roam over every inch of me.

The pressure is back, pressing harder, growing with every touch until I feel like I'm going to burst. I keep my eyes locked on Liam, try to memorize every single detail so I can remember him forever. Raw, masculine, barely controlled as he grips the doorframe with his other hand, muscles straining as he strokes faster.

"God, Aislinn."

I shatter. Waves of sensation swamp my body as I press my hand against my core and cry out his name.

He growls, yanking his pants up a moment before he grunts my name and his body shudders with his release.

My body collapses back into onto the bed, and my eyes drift shut. Delicious warmth flows through me, leaves me feeling sated and blissfully weak. That was more satisfying than anything I've experienced in my entire life.

The door clicks shut. I smile, anticipation making my skin pebble.

But all I hear is the howling of the wind.

I open my eyes and look over. My door is shut. I sit up and look around, my heart starting to pound against my ribs.

Liam is gone.

I don't know how long I sit there in the dark. Emotions try to worm their way in: mortification, grief, anger, regret. I choose numbness, wrap it around my almost naked body like a blanket.

I keep telling myself I can handle this. But it's become painfully obvious that I can't.

Starting tomorrow, I'm going to keep my distance from Liam. It'll hurt, but it's the best thing for both of us. And once we get back to New York, I'm going to find somewhere else to stay while I live out the terms of our agreement. We can't be alone together.

That more than anything nearly breaks down my walls. Once I could go over to Liam's penthouse and relax on his couch with a movie and popcorn. I could even sleep over if I had an event the next morning that was closer to his place than my apartment.

Now we can't even be in the same room without setting each other on fire.

I pull my top back up and wiggle back into my shorts and underwear. I crawl under the covers, burrowing deep beneath the fleece.

For one moment, I let myself think *what if.* What if Liam could let himself feel again, fall in love with me? What if he did want to get married? Have a family?

And then I push the thoughts away. I've already made plenty of mistakes in this marriage. I'm not about to make the worst mistake of all and let myself hope for a future with Liam.

CHAPTER FIFTEEN

Aislinn

THE WORLD IS still white. Endless white, as far as I can see. But unlike last night, or rather early this morning with the snow swirling in the wind and the howling storm, the day is calm. The storm is gone. Gray clouds lay like a thick blanket above, but I can still separate land from sky, can still see the fjord below our cliff and the mountains surrounding us.

Whoever manages the villa left a pair of binoculars in the living room, as well as a book about the different kinds of wildlife in the area. A quick look confirms that the road leading from the villa to the main highway is covered in snow.

I set my mug of tea down on the counter. I've never enjoyed giving myself pleasure as much as I did last night. But every time I woke up, it was like I hadn't found any release. Instead, there was an ache, one that deepened every time I thought about his eyes burning into mine, his hand stroking up and down his cock, him growling my name…

I pick up the tea and chug it, wincing as it burns my

tongue. At least it gives me something else to focus on besides the pulsing between my thighs.

My phone buzzes. I roll my eyes at the notification of yet another news article, then stop as I catch one of the words in the title.

...philanthropist...

Confused, I click the link. There are the usual photos of Liam and me, some from the opera house and some from our time out and about in Reykjavik. The vultures are speculating about where we've gone for the next part of our honeymoon.

But farther down is a paragraph about Liam. It mentions his donations to a foster support program, a mentorship network for teenagers in care, and something called the Carpenter School. My finger trembles as I click on the link for the school. My eyes grow hot as I read aloud.

"Established five years ago by Liam Whitlock in honor of his parents, Robert and Norrine. To give the next generation a chance at a future."

He's never once mentioned any of this. From the little I can dig up, his support has been almost exclusively financial. No public appearances, no fancy galas. Just Liam giving money to causes he believes in.

I shove my phone back in my pocket and stand. Every time I turn around, there's a new layer to uncover, another aspect to the man I thought I knew so well. His time in foster care, the impact his adoptive parents' death had on him, his feelings about his birth mother... And now this, a generosity he won't let anyone else see. Another layer that deepens the emotional love I haven't been able to shake myself free of.

Coupled with our experience last night, I'm in deep trouble.

Restless, frantic energy propels me into the living room. The desire Liam has ignited in me is strong—too strong. It was so much easier loving him from afar, entertaining the occasional daydream about what life could be like. I never allowed myself the fantasy of imagining what it would be like to kiss him, to go to bed with him. Entertaining dreams like that only made it hurt worse when I saw him with a date on his arm.

But now, with each passing day, our friendship is receding as this new dynamic takes root. Which means that even after all I've done to protect Liam and Diana, I'll still lose him in the end. After what we shared last night, there's no going back to being just friends. Or moving forward, either.

I stare out over the swells of snow. Do I wish Liam would change his mind about a family? Fall in love with me and ask me to marry him? Yes. But I will never ask that of him. I won't be like William Luther and tell him to change himself so I can accept him.

God, I need to get out—away from the house, away from sharing a roof with Liam.

I grab a sleek binder off the coffee table that has all the information about the villa. I open it to the amenities page and run my finger down the list of activities the villa has to offer: on-site hot spring-fed mineral bath, gym on the lower level, snowshoes, skis, snowmobiles, sledding, archery.

The mineral bath would be relaxing. But it would still be in the house, where I might glimpse Liam at any time. Same for the gym. I've never tried snowshoeing before. Archery would be impossible with the wind. It's not as bad as yesterday, but Liam received a text message that the winds are gusting hard enough at the airport to prevent the helicopter from taking off. Skiing is an experience I'd rather forget. Nothing like falling flat on your face and knocking a tooth loose in front of a group of US senators.

But snowmobiling… It's been a while since I've driven one. Over two years, I admit with a grimace, when Eric and Stephanie took me on a weeklong getaway to Colorado. That had been around the time Liam had been dating an ice-skating champion and pictures of them kissing after one of her competitions had been splashed all over the news, with one article speculating the skater just might be the one to tame Liam into marriage.

I'd spent hours on the snowmobile, navigating the trails around the log cabin as I tried to keep my mind on nature and off the image of Liam with his arms around another woman. It had taken awhile, but eventually I'd found my rhythm with the snowmobile, alternating between speeding around curves and gliding down long stretches of trail. Exhilarating at times, peaceful at others.

I need the peace more than anything right now.

Decision made, I snap a photo of the recommended routes. The trails themselves will be covered, but the landmarks noted on the map will still be visible. The wind will make things interesting, but I want to get out.

Have to get out.

I hurry back to my bedroom, grateful when I make it without seeing Liam.

A couple minutes later I'm in the garage, bundled up in thick, fleece-lined winter gear. The snowmobile is brand-new, with a sleek frame and wide skis that will make navigating the recent snowfall a breeze. Excited, I grab the oversize dolly at the back of the garage and maneuver it into place before pushing the snowmobile outside.

The air is ice-cold. I breathe it in, savoring the clean taste of it as I straddle the snowmobile and turn the key. The engine hums to life.

"What the hell are you doing?"

I was so close. So close to freedom.

I glance at the throttle. Maybe I should just hop on and gun it. There's only one snowmobile. It's not like he could catch me anytime soon.

Except I didn't grab the helmet yet. Damn it.

Slowly, I turn and look up.

Liam is glaring down at me from the deck above.

"Going for a ride."

"By yourself?"

I grit my teeth. "Yes."

"Without telling me?"

Okay, that part was stupid. "Hey. I'm going snowmobiling."

"Not without me, you're not."

Oh yes, let's add the hot hunk of a man I can barely keep my hands off to the back of my snowmobile and have him intimately pressed against me on an hour-long ride. That'll cool me off.

"No."

"It wasn't a question, Aislinn."

"I've been snowmobiling before."

"I don't care."

I explode. "Damn it, Liam, I'm a grown woman. I don't need a babysitter."

"I'm fully aware you're a grown woman—"

"So leave me alone." Tears prick the backs of my eyes.

Horrified, I look down. He's already seen me in one vulnerable position. I can't handle crying in front of him, too.

I look away and stalk into the garage. I grab a helmet off the shelf and am nearly back at the snowmobile when Liam runs out the door in the same black silky pants from last night and a T-shirt.

My mouth drops open. "Where's your coat?"

"I'm a grown man," he fires back. "Aislinn, we need to talk—"

"I don't want to talk! I just want..." I gesture out toward the snow-covered fields. "I just want to go. I want to be away from this house and away from you and us and what happened last night, and I—"

Liam reaches out and grabs my arm. "Then let me go with you. Make sure you stay safe."

I force out a laugh. "God, even after all this time, that's all you can see me as, isn't it? Poor little Aislinn with her head in the clouds. I can't tell a lamb from a wolf. Too foolish to see the bad in the world." I wrench my arm out of his grasp. "Like I said, Liam, I grew up. I'm not the stupid girl you once knew."

Liam stares at me. "Stupid?"

"Yes," I snap. "And guess what, you were right. The world is dark, and the people you love and trust can betray you without ever blinking an eye." A tear slips out, and God, it's cold. "I'm not perfect, but I'm not weak like I was."

"Would you stop?" He grips both my arms and hauls me close to him. "I have never once thought you were stupid or weak, Aislinn. Not once."

I blink. "But...you always said..."

"I always said I worried that people would take advantage of your kind heart. I never thought you were weak because of it, Aislinn." He leans down, his breath feathering across my face. "You were stronger for it. Stronger than I could ever be."

The world tilts. I open my mouth, but no words come out.

"I want to come with you because you've never been snowmobiling in Iceland before. We're snowed in. The helicopter can't take off, so an air evacuation is out if you get hurt. I'd rather not risk you getting injured and me spending hours looking for you."

All rational arguments. Ones I didn't consider when I came up with my brilliant plan, which unfortunately reinforces his point.

"Give me five minutes to get dressed?"

I nod, not trusting myself to speak.

"We need to talk about last night. But," he adds softly as I tense, "later. Let's just enjoy the moment."

He's back in less than three. I climb on the snowmobile, forcing myself not to react when he gets on behind me. As soon as I press down on the throttle and start forward, my rear slides back. His legs are on either side of me, his body cradling me as I navigate us through the snow.

I don't know exactly when it happens, but at some point, I start to relax. My body is still acutely aware of Liam sitting behind me. But with patches of blue sky peeking through the clouds and pale beams of sun making the snow glitter, it's hard to hold on to the turmoil that drove me out of the villa and into the snow.

I've seen snow before, mountains and lakes. But Iceland is raw, untamed in a way I've never seen before.

The snowmobile skims over the snow. Off to my right, steam rises from one of the things on the map. We pass by and continue on to where a lone pine tree stands tall and proud. I pull the snowmobile under its thick branches and turn it off.

"We shouldn't go too far toward the mountain." I nod my head in the direction of a soaring peak. "About a hundred feet that way, the cliff drops off into the fjord." I stand and shake out my hair.

"When did you learn how to drive a snowmobile?"

I glance over my shoulder. Liam is standing just a few feet away, his helmet in one hand and his balaclava in the other. His hair is messy, like someone has just run their fingers through it.

God knows I'd like to.

I mentally curse as I turn and face the mountain again. "A couple of years ago. Eric and Stephanie took me to Colorado. I spent most of the week exploring the trails."

Snow crunches softly behind me. I tense, all too aware of how close Liam is when he stops just behind me.

"He should have stood by you."

Hurt gnashes through me, but I shrug. "He had bigger things to worry about."

I always hated the term *greater good*. Except I, too, chose the greater good over doing what was inherently right. How can I possibly judge when I also made decisions I never thought myself capable of? When I've let Eric's misdeeds go unpunished all these months?

An ugly, wicked thought winds itself around my lungs and squeezes. If Liam knew that I'd kept Eric's secret to ensure the passing of the bill, that I continued to keep it because of my own inner conflicts, would he still see me as someone good and kind? Or would he turn away from me?

I hear Liam's soft inhale, as if he's about to say something else. Something moves to my left, a quick flash of white on white. I turn and gasp.

There, standing in the snow, is a fox—brilliant white fur speckled with gray, large, inquisitive eyes fixed on Liam and me.

I grab Liam's arm and squeeze. "Look."

I don't know how long we stand there, but finally, the fox turns its head and slowly pads through the snow. It pauses every now and then, sniffing the ground, even hopping up into the air a couple of times. Just as it's about ready to disappear beyond the hill, something else moves to my right. Another fox bounds across the snow, its stride long and its movements almost happy. It runs up to the first fox, gives it a gentle nuzzle with its snout, and then the two turn and disappear over the hill.

My breath comes out in a rush. "Did you see that?"

"I did." He sounds amused, but I don't care.

"That was amazing!" Even when I was in Colorado, the only animals I saw were deer. But an arctic fox?

I move out from beneath the tree and crane my neck up toward the sky. The clouds are rapidly disappearing, leaving a blanket of brilliant blue above. "This place is incredible."

Liam

She's stunning. Absolutely beautiful. How did I not see her before?

"Incredible," she repeats again as she turns in a slow circle. Her eyes sparkle. Roses bloom in her cheeks. Her hair falls in messy golden strands around her face. Even in her puffy jacket and snow pants, her hands encased in fur-lined gloves, she's the sexiest woman I've ever laid my eyes on.

"Last night."

Her joy disappears almost instantly. She goes still, almost like the fox we just saw. Wary, trapped. "I thought we were going to enjoy ourselves."

"We are," I say quietly. "I'm enjoying this."

"I was."

My mouth tilts up into a grin. Never in my life did I picture Aislinn being sassy. But God, I enjoy it.

"What is there to talk about?"

My amusement disappears as I stare at her. "You're joking, right?"

"Look, we talked about this. We're friends helping each other out. A relationship wasn't supposed to cross that far into intimacy, but it did. So let's chalk it up as an accident and move on."

"An accident?" I repeat. "That was no accident."

"Oh. So you walked into my room on purpose? Did you know…" Her voice trails off. She clears her throat. "Did you know what I was doing in there?"

It's twenty degrees outside, but it might as well be in the hundreds on a tropical island with how quickly heat swamps me.

"I came to check on you. I heard you moaning. I assumed you were sick or hurt. So yes, I opened the door."

I nearly swallowed my tongue. When I saw her stretched out on her bed, nearly naked, one hand capped around her full breast, the other buried between her legs, my body went so hard I wouldn't have been able to move from her doorway even if I'd tried.

"No, I didn't know. I would never violate your privacy like that."

She looks down. "I'm sorry. That was unfair." She shakes her head. "I've been unfair to you a lot."

It would be easy to go down that path, to ask her why she's been pushing me away ever since that night of the gala. But I'm not about to be distracted now.

"I didn't know," I repeat, "but I'm damn glad I opened that door."

Her head snaps up. She stares at me, her eyes wide. "What?"

I walk toward her, much like I did the first day we arrived here—slow, measured steps. She's tense, frozen. But she stands her ground. I keep walking until nothing separates us but a sliver of winter air.

"I have never seen anything sexier or more beautiful than the sight of you touching yourself."

Her lips part. "You don't mean that."

"I do."

Her eyes drift down towards my mouth. She leans in. I tilt my head down, my body hard, ready to feel her lips—

She puts a hand to my chest. Firm, flat. "I need a moment."

Every fiber of my being is on fire. Demanding I kiss her again, take things further, deeper. Claim her. But I have no idea how she feels about all this. Yes, it was my name on her lips last night when she came. And God willing, before this honeymoon is over, I'll know what her body feels like wrapped around my cock.

But I'm not going to push her. When she comes to my bed, it's because she won't be able to fight this attraction between us any longer.

I should be fighting it. But that ship has sailed. I can't

fight it anymore. Not after seeing her laid bare and just out of reach.

"We should get back." She blinks, shakes her head slightly. "Liam—we've been out for a while. It's cold. Let's not push it."

She's been pushed and bullied enough. I still don't know why she married Dexter, although I've got a pretty damn good idea, and it wasn't willingly. Still so many pieces to sort through. But we have a couple of days here, at least, not to mention the rest of our marriage.

I glance at her out of the corner of my eye as we walk back toward the snowmobile. When we first agreed to the terms of our marriage, three and a half years seemed like a long time to play being in love, committed.

But now, as Aislinn pulls on her helmet and throws one leg over the snowmobile, it suddenly doesn't seem that long at all.

CHAPTER SIXTEEN

Aislinn

I WALK DOWN the hall to the bedroom Liam claimed as his own. Nerves flutter in my stomach, but I keep going.

After we got back from our ride, Liam helped me get the snowmobile in the garage and then disappeared inside. I went to my room and took a long, hot shower. At first, I just focused on the blazing water on my back, the steam clouding the room.

But as I scrubbed soap up and down my legs, my hands drifting over my breasts, I made a choice. One that absolutely terrified me. But after what Liam had told me by the tree, the way he looked at me, I know I will always regret it if I don't take this step.

I stop at Liam's door, sucking in a deep breath, and knock.

Footsteps sound on the other side, then Liam opens the door. "Aislinn…" His voice trails off as his eyes drop down, going from passive to burning in an instant when he realizes all I'm wearing is a towel.

"I want you, too."

The words are barely out of my mouth before he's hauling me against him.

His mouth fuses to mine. I moan against his lips as his fingers dig into my hips. He bands one arm around my waist and drags me inside, kicking the door shut behind us. We move to the bed, hands frantic, breath mingling.

I step back long enough to drop the towel. The towel falls to the floor, leaving me completely naked.

Liam stares at me, his eyes moving over my body with an intimate thoroughness that thrills me to my toes. "How did I not see you?"

Before I can respond, Liam picks me up in his arms, kissing me senseless as he turns and lays me down gently, then covers my body with his. His hands are on my back, then gliding up my sides, cupping my breasts with an exquisite tenderness that brings tears to my eyes.

"Liam," I murmur against his mouth.

Liam lifts his head.

I freeze. Is he going to pull away again?

"You're so beautiful, Aislinn." He leans down and brushes his lips against the swell of my breast.

My eyes flutter shut as I moan. It feels so good, the wet heat of his mouth on my skin, the teasing touch of his fingers as his hands shift down to my waist. When he scrapes his teeth over my nipple, I tense. When he sucks my nipple into his mouth, I cry out. Each caress of his lips, his tongue, heightens the sensation from through my body. I thread my fingers through his hair, hold on as he shifts to the other breast.

His mouth is fire on my skin. Did I think my own hands could even begin to compare to what Liam is capable of? He trails kisses down the sides of my breasts, beneath, kissing sensitive skin no one else has. I stare down at him, momentarily jolted by the site of my friend, the man I've loved for so long, kissing me in ways I never thought possible.

And then his mouth moves lower, over my stomach and farther down. My breath starts coming in short, frantic gasps as he captures my hips in his hands. His breath fans over my core, cool and soothing as I restlessly shift my legs.

"Please, Liam. Please."

His chuckle reverberates across my skin. And then he lowers his head, tracing his tongue up and down the seam of my most intimate skin.

Then he feasts. Kisses, licks, teases with the faintest scrape of his teeth that drives me wild.

I reach down, finally tangle my fingers in his hair and press his mouth deeper. "Liam!"

His name comes out on a sob. I can feel myself spiraling up, shooting toward something I've never experienced before. He's relentless, driving me higher, finding every vulnerability I have and exploiting it with his mouth. I come apart, arching into his touch and screaming as pleasure fills me, pours out of me.

Gradually, I come back down to earth. I give a half-hearted laugh mixed with a groan as he presses one last kiss to my skin before sliding up my body.

I peel open my eyes to see him propped up on his elbows above me. "You," I say as I trail a hand down his chest, "are overdressed."

He smirks and pushes himself up onto his knees. I watch as he grabs the hem of his shirt and whips it over his head.

"Better?"

"Getting there."

He rolls off the bed and rids himself of his pants and boxers. I swallow hard at the size of his cock. Thick, hard. He wants me. He really, truly wants me.

He joins me on the bed again. He starts to lower himself on to me, but I stop him with a hand on his chest.

"My turn."

He huffs out a laugh even as I push him onto his back. "Not what I expected."

I pause. None of this is what I expected. I never imagined when I saw Liam just two weeks ago that we would end up in bed together after all these years.

"Hey."

I blink, focus on his face.

He reaches out, traces a finger down my cheek. "You don't—"

I lean down and flick my tongue against the tip of his hardness.

He groans, his hips arching up. "Tease."

I smile at him before sliding my mouth down his length. I love the way his body moves beneath my hands, love the taste of him, the feel of him as I both give pleasure and take it with every moan, every muffled curse.

"Enough." He sits up, grabs me by my arms and has me on my back within seconds. "I need you, Aislinn."

My throat tightens. For years, I just wanted to be wanted for myself. And now, in this moment, I finally am. "I want you, too, Liam."

He suddenly freezes. "Damn it. Condom."

"I'm on the pill. And I'm clean. I haven't…" Embarrassed, I shift beneath him. "It's been a couple years."

He stares down at me. "Years?"

Slowly, I nod.

"It's been over a year for me, too," he says softly. "I've never not used a condom before."

I have no right to feel relieved. But I do. To know that it's been so long makes me feel special. There will be other women after me. But for right now, Liam is mine.

"I want you," I repeat. I reached down between our bodies and grab his cock.

He presses himself against me, his cock hard against my wetness. He slowly slides himself in, stretching me, filling me up. I moan his name, my hands traveling up and down his back as he eases his full length inside me.

"God, Aislinn, you're so tight."

We quickly find a rhythm, our hips moving together as the pleasure builds once more. We whisper each other's names, our fingers stroking, pressing, urging each other onward.

"Liam… God, I can't…"

"Let go, Aislinn. Just let go."

I do, coming on a scream as I clench my legs down around his waist.

His thrusts grow deeper, harder, and then he arches back and groans. "Aislinn."

Warm heat fills me. I wrap my arms around him, arch my neck as he presses his face against my skin and kisses me.

My eyes drift shut. Between our excursion and the incredible lovemaking, I'm exhausted. The bed shifts. A moment later I'm covered by a thick blanket.

"Sweet dreams, Aislinn."

I drift off to sleep, dreaming of Liam and me dancing in the snow, oblivious to the storm gathering on the horizon.

CHAPTER SEVENTEEN

Aislinn

I WAKE UP SLOWLY. Warm sunlight fills the room. My eyes are open long enough to see the curtains pulled and a fire still flickering in the hearth.

A hot, heavy arm slides across my waist.

Liam.

He presses a soft, tender kiss to my cheek. I turn and look at him. Is this even possible?

"Good morning." His voice rumbles through me. So familiar, yet so different as we lie there, naked in bed.

"Good morning."

His smile is slow and languid. Satisfied. And given that he woke me up around midnight and made love to me again, I'm not surprised.

"How do you feel?"

"Tender. Sleepy." I smile shyly. "Happy."

His smirk disappears as he leans in and kisses me.

My body responds instantly. I roll over and straddle his hips, brazenly rubbing myself against his rapidly hardening cock.

"Aislinn," he groans.

I grab him with bold confidence, angle myself and then sink deep down, moaning as he fills me.

His hands clamp down on my thighs like a vice. "Ride me."

I move up and down, need coursing through me as he fills me. I cup my breasts, gently tug on my nipples.

"Fuck, yes," he groans. "I love watching you touch yourself."

I move faster, sinking down even deeper, watching the play of emotions across his face. He's so handsome. So sexy. A man who knows me far better than anyone else.

A man I love and will always love, even if he can never love me back.

Liam thrusts his hips upward. My orgasm hits, sends me spiraling over the edge. Liam follow the moment later, filling me with his heat.

I slump forward on his chest.

He chuckles into my hair. "Good morning."

"You already said that."

"Well, now I'm saying it again." He presses a kiss to my hair.

I scrunch my eyes tight. This is far more than I ever thought I would have with him. Yes, in a few days we'll go back to reality. But I need to take this gift I've been given and make the most of it.

"Are you all right?" He's watching me, alert and curious. Perhaps even suspicious.

"Yes. Just overthinking things."

His face softens. "Let's get breakfast."

We bundle into our robes and walk down the hallway. He grabs my hand halfway down the hall, wrapping his fingers tightly around mine. He makes quick work of pulling out various dishes left by the catering company: bagels piled high with thick slices of lox and topped off with dill and capers. Skyr, Icelandic yogurt that could classify as a dessert with its thick creaminess, topped with honey and frozen raspberries. Rich, thick coffee that makes me moan as he sets a cup in front of me.

"How am I ever going to go back to breakfast burritos?"

Liam chuckles as he scoops up a spoonful of yogurt. "We could always eat like this back home."

I nearly drop my fork. "Yeah. That sounds nice."

"Okay," Liam says. "What's going on?"

I set my fork down, put my elbows on the table and scrub my hands over my face. "I feel...uncomfortable."

His face sharpens. "With me?"

"No. With me. Myself." My heart starts to pound. "You keep telling me I'm this amazing person. That I'm strong and good."

"You are strong and good."

I lay my palms flat on the countertop, steel myself. "But what if I'm not?"

Liam sets his spoon down and leans back in his chair.

I resist the urge to squirm under his gaze. Why did I bring this up? Because of the guilt I felt yesterday while we were snowmobiling? We were having a pleasant morning. And what if after he hears the truth my worst fear comes true? What if after I've finally gotten to be with Liam he pulls away? "Maybe we shouldn't talking about this."

"No." He shakes his head. "You can't run from this, Aislinn."

Hurt spears through me. "Is that what you think I did? Ran away?"

"I don't know. I don't know, because you never once

reached out for help. You never told Diana or me anything. You just disappeared."

"I wasn't…" I sigh. "I wasn't thinking. I was stupid."

"Stop saying that," Liam snaps. "You're one of the smartest people I know. Look at Eric's campaign before and after you came on board. You took his career and turned it into a powerhouse. Yes, he's done good work, but you're the one who told his story, told the story of the people whose lives he changed. You're not just smart, but you know people. You open yourself up to them, and they, in turn, open up to you." He leans forward, eyes blazing. "How could you ever think that was a weakness?"

"And what if Eric wasn't who we thought he was? What if he did something bad?" My throat grows thick. "What if he did all of these good things, but he's still a selfish person?"

Liam's face softens. "You married Dexter to protect Eric."

Slowly, I nod.

"Aislinn. Why didn't you come to me? To Diana?"

"Because he threatened you, too."

Liam's face hardens, his eyes going ice-cold.

A shiver creeps down my spine as I remember the way he pummeled Diana's adoptive father. I have no doubt that if Dexter were still alive, Liam would be planning a way to hunt him down and hold him accountable.

"He threatened to tank your firm, to ruin Diana's career. He knew so many people, had so many people's secrets in the palm of his hand…" I suck in a shuddering breath. "But at least I learned a valuable lesson."

"What?" Liam snaps. "That people screw up? That sometimes the world's not perfect?"

Angry, I turn and face the mountain again. "You don't understand."

"What don't I understand? We've led different lives, but I know what it's like to lose, to be disappointed, to be hurt."

"And what about used?" I face him again, my hands curled into fists at my sides. "What if every single person in your life wanted you, not because of who you were, but because of what you could do for them? And what if you spent your whole life thinking that one day, one day, it would get better? And you pretended like your adoptive father didn't adopt you because it looked good for his reelection campaign? And your adoptive mother went along with it because she was the dutiful wife and wanted to make her husband happy? What if the first time I was proposed to was because a madman wanted to use me and my connection to my father to further his own ambitions? And what if—"

My voice trails off. I'm angry. So angry. But I don't want to hurt Liam.

"What if one of your best friends proposed to you for a business arrangement?" Liam finishes quietly.

We stand there, the only sounds the occasional whisper of the wind or snow falling from the trees onto the ground.

"Is Stephanie involved, too?"

The pain cuts deeper. Eric's distance stung, but he still gave me so much. Stephanie, on the other hand, had been what I'd always dreamed of—a mother. Until I saw her signature on several of the documents Dexter had kept. I can't see a scenario where she's not involved in some way, no matter how badly I want things to be different.

Maybe I'm making excuses for myself, but when I made those choices, it was with the thought of protecting a bill that would, in turn, protect thousands of children. What Stephanie and Eric did only benefited themselves.

"I don't know. We haven't talked much since everything happened."

"Why did you decide to keep Eric a secret?"

"We had been working on that bill for years. Years," I repeat. "It's something that should have been discussed and passed within hours. That's not the way the system works, but it should."

Frustrated, I stand and start to pace. "I know that's my idealistic self talking. But it just doesn't make sense. This should be a no-brainer. Dexter must have done his homework on me because he knew how important the bill was to me. He knew how involved I was and threatened to make sure it would never get passed." I snort. "God only knows how many other senators and legislators he had in his pocket."

"So you concealed your adoptive father's breach of ethics to ensure that foster kids would grow up in better environments?"

It sounds so cut and dry. "I did it for the children, so it must be okay, right?"

"So what's holding you back from accepting that?"

"Because I still did it. I still made a choice. A choice to lie, to conceal, and not about something small. And as soon as I kept that lie, then another took its place. I pretended like I was falling for Dexter. I shut you and Diana out. I told Eric and Stephanie everything was okay. And Stephanie asked a lot." My lips curve up into a sad smile. "I always told myself, even when I was little, that even though I didn't have a family, I had myself. Rules, beliefs to live by. That even if no one wanted me at the end of the day, I could still be true to myself." I finally look at him. "And now I don't even know who I am anymore."

Liam stands and circles the table. "In all the years I've known you, I never realized how high of a standard you hold yourself to. But it's okay that you're not perfect, Aislinn. No one is."

"I know that. I make mistakes, but this..." I grab the folds of my robe and pull them tightly together at the base of my neck. Hiding. Shielding. "I hated him, Liam. I hated him, and when I found him, I was glad he was dead." Tears pour down my cheeks. "Who thinks like that? What kind of person is happy that someone else's life is over?"

"He abused you, Aislinn." Liam slowly reaches out.

When I don't pull away, he tugs me closer until I'm standing in the circle of his arms.

"He manipulated and used you. He was willing to sacrifice all the children that would have benefited from that bill for his own personal gain." He leans back, looks down at me. "And you still gave him respect. He'd earned none of it, but you gave him a funeral, a wake. You never once disparaged him to anyone." He presses a gentle kiss to my forehead. "You're human, Aislinn. And in this case, I wouldn't even say that you made a mistake. You went through something horrific. You had difficult choices to make. If I had been in your shoes, I would have probably made the same ones."

My lips tremble as I barely manage to hold in my sobs. Finally telling someone everything, having him hear my darkest secrets and still be standing in front of me, takes the weight off my heart. "Thank you."

He tucks a strand of hair behind my ear. "Don't let Dexter take away who you are." He lays a hand over my chest. "You are kind, Aislinn. And yes, now you've seen that you can be harsh. But you know it can be good, too. And the second that you stop believing in that and fighting for it, that's when Dexter will win."

He's right. It's going to be hard, opening back up. There was something so easy about not feeling much of anything.

Liam's smile chases away the last lingering clouds. "Something I have noticed is your confidence."

"Oh?"

"Before, you would always tiptoe around, making sure everyone felt heard, seen." His teeth flash white as his grin widens. "The Aislinn I've seen the last few weeks stands up for herself."

"Still diplomatic—unless it's you," I joke, half teasing, half apologetic.

"True. But it's good, Aislinn. You're important, too."

I breathe in. For the first time in over a year, there's no pressure on my chest, no tightness in my lungs. I'm finally breathing again.

CHAPTER EIGHTEEN

Liam

THE MOON HAS turned the landscape into silver. Stars dot the night sky with tiny drops of light. I'm sitting in the mineral bath just outside Aislinn's bedroom. The water is hot, a sharp contrast to the cold on my shoulders. Champagne bubbles in flutes perched on the stone wall that circles the bath. Overhead, a shooting star streaks across the sky. The perfect honeymoon.

Except our honeymoon was never supposed to be like this. Two friends selling a story to the public, her to recoup a public image, me to establish a private one. But now that I've had her, seen her, I can't get enough of her.

After her confession this morning, we finished breakfast before I sweet-talked her into taking a shower. By the end of it, I had her facing the wall, hands braced on the tile, my hands on her hips again as I drove myself inside her.

I forced myself to stay away after breakfast while I answered emails and reviewed expenses for the office. Prepping for the opening has consumed my attention for well over a year. But just receiving an email from her halfway through the morning with a detailed public relations campaign made me crave her. The sight of her name made me hard.

Reading the details on what she proposed, a campaign that seamlessly blended high-end luxury with subtle outreaches to communities in need, made me want to see her, talk to her.

The woman is brilliant. How had I not ever talked with her about my plans for my business?

And then I came face-to-face with the ugly realization that I hadn't shared because my business was an extension of myself, of my own dreams and desires rooted in years of pain. Yet another piece I hadn't been willing to share.

I forwarded her recommendations to my head of public relations and requested a check made out to my wife for consultation services. A check, I thought with a smile, she'd probably argue with me over. And damned if I wasn't looking forward to that argument, to silencing her with a kiss and…

I stopped that thought process, shaken at how easy it was to suddenly see Aislinn in my future. Was I actually contemplating this? Contemplating something more with a woman I used to refer to as my little sister?

How can I offer her a future when the thing she wants the most—a family—is something I'm not capable of?

Except as I sat at my desk and thought about Aislinn, thought about her with a child in her lap or a baby in her arms, the longing that flared in Reykjavik dug deep into my skin. It was unsettling to consider that the things I told myself I wasn't capable of having or didn't want are all things I might have just pushed away out of fear.

I turned back to my work and made it one more hour after her email.

She was in the living room, wrapped up in a pile of blankets, watching a movie. I joined her, and we spent the rest of the afternoon lounging on the couch and indulging in the high-end snacks left by the caterers: handcrafted chocolate truffles, gourmet popcorn with real flecks of gold.

I took advantage of her lying in my arms to let my hands wander beneath her shirt, tease the waistband of her pants. But there were also long stretches of time where I was content to simply hold her, listen to her laugh at the movie or murmur an observation.

I can't recall the last time I felt so satisfied with a romantic partner. All of my previous relationships have been rooted in sex and mutual interest in physical pleasure that, once gone, meant the end of the relationship.

But I don't think I would ever lose that with Aislinn.

The thought of not having her in my life, being with someone else at some point in the distant future, makes me sick. And the thought of her with someone else, another man holding her hand, kissing her cheek, daring to touch a single hair on her body, has me wanting to punch something.

Careful.

Part of the reason I shy away from emotions is simply because I don't want to get hurt again. But part of it is because I've also seen what I'm capable of. Punching my first foster brother in the face was just the tip of the iceberg. What I did to Diana's foster father, even though it was ruled in defense of someone else, was confirmation that emotions can be violent, unpredictable.

Dangerous.

We only have one more day, maybe two at the most. The winds have finally died down enough for the helicopter to take off, only for one of the machine's parts to break. A new part is on its way, and there are no more storms in the forecast.

Twenty-four hours until we leave our unexpected paradise and confront the real world again.

Movement catches my eye.

Aislinn opens the sliding glass door of her suite and steps out onto the patio, bundled up in her thick white robe. She walks over to the bath, her shoulders hunched against the cold. "Please tell me that water is boiling hot."

I arch my brow at her. "Come in and find out."

She stops at the edge of the water. She closes her eyes, takes a deep breath and yanks on the belt of her robe. The robe parts.

My mouth dries at the sight of her in a red one-piece swimsuit with a deep V-neck that gives me a very generous view of the sides of her breasts.

"Cold. Cold." She darts toward the stairs and enters the water, letting out a hiss as she descends. She sinks down until just her head is above the surface. "That's better."

I smile as she drifts over to me. Since we talked this morning, she's been happier. More like herself, but still with that edge of confidence I see. I hand her a glass of champagne.

She sits next to me, her thigh brushing mine, and tilts the glass up. "That's delicious." She tilts her head back and looks up at the stars. "Do you think we'll see the Northern Lights? Ari says there's a good possibility. And Diana saw them on the southern coast. She said it was the most amazing thing she's ever seen." Aislinn glances at me. "Thank you, by the way. For what you and Diana did. I just wish it would have worked the way I had intended." She shakes her head. "My best guess is that Dexter didn't tell me about your supposed engagement because he knew the chances were high of me reaching out, even though he told me not to."

I think back to that morning when Dexter opened Aislinn's door, when I assumed he'd just left her bed. The rage I felt that morning takes on a new meaning as I sit next to her, my fingers stroking over her bare back. Even then, I felt something for her.

I'm just not sure what to do about it.

The thought of not having Aislinn in my life like this, from the mind-blowing sex to these casual, intimate moments I've never had with another lover, seems impossible. Yet marriage, a real marriage, doesn't feel right. Not when I can't open up and fully be the man she deserves. Not when she wants a family.

"Can I ask you something?" Aislinn murmurs softly.

"Yes."

"If you had all the money and all the prestige in the world, what would you do?"

I smile. "Anything's on the table?"

"Yes."

I sit there for a moment. "When I was seven, I wanted to be a firefighter. The dream of many little boys. And when I was nine, I wanted to be a carpenter."

"A carpenter?" she repeats.

"Yeah. Like my dad. Every time I smell sawdust, I think of him. I remember the row of wooden carvings I kept in my room—toys Dad crafted for me over the years. Toys that were lost when I was put into foster care."

"What were they like?"

"Some of the kindest people I've ever met. They would have loved you."

Aislinn's smile flashes white in the darkness. "From what little you've said, they sound like amazing people."

"They were." I pause. "The boy I was before they died and the man their deaths forced me to become are two very different people."

Aislinn lays her head on my shoulder. The simple contact releases some of the tension from my body. "I'm so sorry."

"I learned quickly that if I cared about what others thought of me, I wouldn't survive foster care. Not emotionally. Once I had the reputation for being angry and sullen, I couldn't shake it. Foster families anticipated it. I didn't help with how I responded to situations, but still, they were automatically reserved and ready to mete out punishment. More than one said I'd amount to nothing."

Aislinn twists so she's looking up at me. I look down to see understanding in her eyes. "And look at you now." She leans up and kisses my jaw.

The simple contact surges through me straight to my heart. "I switched myself off. Apathy kept me stable. I worked toward my goals of becoming independent, of achieving the kind of success that meant I would never have to depend on anyone again."

For a moment, Aislinn is silent. Then, she speaks. "You never really answered my question. Firefighter? Carpenter? Karaoke singer?"

"I actually really enjoy what I do. Helping people build their own wealth is immensely satisfying."

She frowns at me. "But you're already working with people who have a lot of money."

"I saw a lot of families struggling during my time in foster care. There were some decent ones, but there were a lot of them that did it for the money. I promised myself

I would never find myself in that position. Once I realized what I could achieve, it just seemed like a no-brainer to reach as high as possible."

Aislinn's frowning at me. "But does it make you happy?"

"Happy?" I repeat.

"All the money. The penthouse."

I start to respond, then stop. *Does it make me happy?*

It's unsettling to realize I don't have a good answer. It should be an unequivocal yes. I made clients millions, and in some case billions, when I worked for the firm. I'm opening my own financial advising practice. My investments have paid off to the point I own a penthouse on Billionaires' Row, a brownstone in one of New York's elite neighborhoods, and I've vacationed all over the world.

But when I think back to what's truly made me happy over the years, the first thing to come to mind is my parents. The second is Aislinn and Diana. People who loved fiercely, who stood up for others gave them a voice. While I hoarded money and climbed corporate ladders, all for the sake of reaching independence. Keeping people as far away as possible.

What would make me happy?

I think back over the past week—even with the tension— I've had some of the happiest moments of my life with Aislinn. Apprehension knots my chest. I don't know when it happened, but at some point, Aislinn became far more than I had ever anticipated. I care about her. Deeply. More than I ever have any other woman.

I've lived most of my life with the conviction that being alone is better.

But I can't remember a happier time in my life than these last few days with her. When I think of my future post-divorce, there's no satisfaction at accomplishing my goal, no relief at returning to my old lifestyle. Instead, there's an ache, a knowledge that one of the best things to ever happen me will no longer be there.

"I don't know." A bald-faced lie, but I don't know how to share yet the conflict inside me.

Thankfully, Aislinn doesn't push. Instead, she grabs my hand under the water and squeezes. "You're a good guy, Liam."

I huff out a laugh. "I'm a selfish bastard."

"Foster Connect. The Big Kids Network. The Carpenter School." She says the name softly.

My muscles tighten with each mention. "What about them?"

"You've been donating to the first two for years. You created the third on your own." Her voice hitches. "A carpentry program for kids aging out of foster care. I didn't realize the connection to your dad until now."

"I give money, Aislinn," I say firmly. "It's not anything close to what you do. The campaign you shared—which my head of publicity thought was phenomenal—wasn't just smart. It had heart, Aislinn. You naturally care, and it shows in your work, just like it shows in what my brother does with his company." I pause. "That's not me."

"So change it." She gently nudges me. "You could use one of those for your charity fundraisers—"

"No," I cut her off. "I don't want to use any of them to help my business."

Her slow smile is sexy, knowing. "Any other man would have jumped at the chance to use those organizations for public relations. But you care."

I shake my head. "You're giving me too much credit."

"That campaign was created based on the work you've

already done, Liam. Yes, you cater to top-tier clients, but you've made impacts with your money. Thoughtful ones. For crying out loud, I know you were the one who gave Mrs. Scout that money when she retired."

I try to look away, but she reaches out and lays a hand on my cheek.

"You don't give yourself enough credit. Maybe it's time to re-evaluate."

"And what about you?"

She blinks like an owl. "Me?"

"You're good at what you do. Great, actually." I lean over and give in to the urge to kiss her cheek. "When are you going to grab your life with both hands and start living again?"

"Well… I did get a job offer from the Foster Foundation."

My whole body tightens. "The ones who rejected you until you suddenly became famous?"

Her shoulders sag. "I know. I just… What if it's my only chance?"

"What would make you happy? Professionally," I clarify.

Aislinn's brows draw together in a frown. "Working in PR. But…" Her smile is slight, shy. "Starting up my own foundation. I wouldn't want to run it, but mold it the way I want it to be run, then make sure it gets the attention it deserves."

I smile. Of course Aislinn's professional goals are tied into something that helps others. "So why not do it?"

She stares at me for a long second, the steam adding a sheen to her skin. Then, slowly, she looks down. "Because I'm afraid." She draws in a deep, shuddering breath. "I've failed so much this past year—"

I reach over, snake my arms around her waist and draw her into my lap. She lets out a soft squeal that drives me crazy. I kiss her hard until she's melting in my arms.

I pull back, smooth a strand of wet hair out of her face.

"You also were the driving force behind a bipartisan bill that is going to help hundreds of thousands of children. You did everything you could…" My voice breaks for a second, and I look down. "You protected me. And Diana." I look back up at her, my chest tight and my throat thick. "I wish you could see yourself the way I see you."

Her eyes are shining, full of emotion that both ensnares and terrifies me. But before I can begin to decipher her emotions and my response, she looks up. Her arms tighten around my neck.

"Liam, look."

The breathless wonder in her voice makes me look up.

Light arcs across the sky, shades of green and violet rippling through the inkiness of night. It almost looks like the tendrils of light are dancing.

My eyes flick to Aislinn. She's staring up, a huge smile on her face and wonder in her eyes.

What if I break her?

Aislinn has been through so much, survived so much. I always thought there would never be a man good enough for her. Over the last twelve years, I did exactly as Aislinn accused me of and took everything she and Diana had to offer, encouraged them to share, to depend on me while I held myself back.

Even now, after everything she's shared, I'm still holding back. Still selfish. Still not wanting to let go of my control and let her in.

I want to be the man for her. But just sharing the bits and pieces I have over the last few days has been like pulling blood from stone. It's hard, unnatural. Yeah, I've donated money. But I haven't done anything of purpose. Nothing that hasn't benefited myself.

Aislinn deserves someone who will match her, who can make her feel just as loved as she'll make them feel. Someone who can see the world the way she does.

Not someone who's world exists solely around himself.

The thought has my hands curling into my fists beneath the water. I want it to be me. But what if the best thing for Aislinn is letting her go?

She turns to me with shining eyes. "I'm so glad I got to share this with you."

I pluck the champagne glass from her fingers and set it on the rocks. I pull her on to my lap, positioning her until she's straddling my legs. I slide my hand up her neck and bury my fingers in her hair. I kiss her deeply, drink her moans.

Her head drops back, exposing her neck to my lips. I slide the straps of her bathing suit down, fill my hands with her breasts as my name comes out on a breathless whisper.

I shift enough to slide my swimsuit down and release my cock. I slide the material of her suit aside and in one long thrust, I fill her. She arches back, calls out my name. I slide my fingers back into her hair, anchor her head and kiss her as I take her.

I make love to her under the stars and the glimmer of the Northern Lights, knowing it will most likely be one of the last times.

CHAPTER NINETEEN

Aislinn

THE PHONE RINGING wakes me. I stretch in bed and roll over. My hand falls on a cool sheet.

I frown and glance around. My room is empty. Liam's phone is on the nightstand. I reach over and grab it. A quick glance at the screen shows it's a local number. Feeling a little guilty, I answer. "Hello?"

"Mrs. Whitlock?"

The small smile that crosses my face is reflexive. It's the first time someone's addressed me by my married name since our wedding day. "Yes."

"This is Bjarki, the villa manager. How have you been holding up?"

I glance at the rumpled sheets and bite down on my lower lip. After making love under the stars, we wandered back inside for a late dessert and more wine.

And more sex.

In the shower just before bed.

In the middle of night when Liam woke me to see the aurora borealis shifting into a spectacular sea of red and violet before sliding into me from behind, one arm pinned around my waist, my back against his chest.

"Really well."

"I'm glad to hear it. And also glad to share that the helicopter is ready."

My heart sinks. "Oh."

"Is that all right?"

"Yes!" I force a smile onto my face, try to infuse some pleasantness into my tone. "Yes, it's just a surprise."

"The winds have died down, and we finally got the part we needed. Would two hours from now give you enough time?"

I look around the room. Two hours. Two more hours of just Liam and me.

It's not nearly enough.

"That sounds great."

"The pilot will meet you behind the villa. I'll call when he's over Akureyri."

I place Liam's phone on the nightstand after we hang up. I realize then it's quiet. No wind, no storms racing down the mountains and barreling across the lava fields. I glance out the window, the same window where just hours before Liam was reflected in the glass, his face just over my shoulder, his lips on my neck as he made love to me in front of the Northern Lights.

Now there's not even a cloud in the sky, just endless blue. The perfect winter day in Iceland.

And I'm miserable.

I don't know what happened last night between the mineral baths and going inside. But I could sense something was off. Even though Liam worshipped me, took his time loving every inch of my body, there was an edge to him. A slight distance.

The door to my room opens. Liam walks in wearing the silky black pants and carrying two steaming cups of coffee. "Good morning."

The upswing in my mood quickly takes a downward turn at his barely there smile, the shuttered expression in his eyes. He hands me the coffee and then turns away.

I cup my hands around the mug. "Bjarki called. I hope you don't mind, but I answered."

He sits down in a chair near the fireplace. "What did he have to say?"

"The helicopter's on its way. Two hours."

Liam's gaze shifts to some point outside the huge glass windows.

I turn and look. My body clenches at the sight of the mineral bath at the end of the patio. Our robes lie in crumpled white heaps next to the stairs, our slippers in a jumbled pile next to them. Snow-covered fields stretch out behind the pool. In the far distance, the lone pine tree stands tall and proud.

"Can you be ready by then?"

I blink furiously. When we first got here, I couldn't wait to leave. Now, I don't want to go. I know what's coming. Have known ever since I made the decision to walk into his room. But God it hurts. "Yes."

He stands, sets his cup down and moves to the bed, sitting on the far end. He might as well be on the other side of the fjord for all the distance it puts between us. "After today…" His voice trails, and he lets out a deep breath. "I've really enjoyed our time together."

How many times, I wonder, has he given this speech? How many other women? "Me, too."

"When we go back to New York, we should abide by the original terms of the agreement."

"No sex."

He blinks at my bluntness. "Yes."

"I agree."

His brows draw together in a slight frown. "You do?"

"You've been clear about your expectations from the beginning, Liam. I'm not going to ask for more."

His lips part. He starts to lean forward, his hand coming up. Hope surges…then splinters into fragments as his fingers curl into a fist and he stands. "All right." He grabs his phone off the nightstand.

I wait until the door closes behind him before I roll onto my stomach, bury my face in my pillow and sob. I cry for myself. I cry for the friendship that will never be the same. I cry for the man I love, the man I wish could see himself as I do.

Thirty minutes later, I walk out into the living room with my suitcase trailing behind me. Liam is standing by the door, dressed in a crisp white shirt and black pants as he talks quietly into his phone.

"All right. Yes, Tuesday. Thank you, Bill."

Bill. William Luther. We haven't even left Iceland yet, and already his focus has shifted back to his work. Back to the reason he married me in the first place.

It's not just the pain of rejection or the sting of finding yet another person who can't let me in. No, it's the hurt of seeing a man like Liam, a man who is smart and intelligent and giving, live his life for the next achievement, the next goal in his never-ending quest to be better, instead of letting himself be happy.

I stop a few feet away. "I'm ready."

He glances up, nods, then looks back down at his phone. "Bjarki called. The helicopter should be here in fifteen minutes."

"All right." I clear my throat. "When we get back to New York, I'd like to move into the brownstone."

Liam's head snaps up. His eyes are narrow, his jaw tight. "What?"

My grip tightens on the handle of my suitcase. "I don't think we should continue to live together in the same house."

"That's not going to work."

"Plenty of couples live separately."

"And what will we do when the tabloids pick up on us living apart?" he snaps.

"Appear in public together." I keep my voice calm. "As long as we play out our roles in front of the camera and whatever functions you need me at, we don't need to live together."

"Why?"

Because I love you. Because sleeping apart from you will feel like a part of me is missing. "It'll be more comfortable for me."

His face darkens. "I make you uncomfortable."

"Not you specifically, but our situation, yes. Have you ever lived with an ex-lover after you broke up?"

The glower on his face gives me my answer. "This is different. We're…" His voice trails off.

"I don't think either of us know what we are anymore."

I will always cherish what Liam and I shared in this villa. What we discovered about each other here in Iceland. But that doesn't mean there won't be moments when I pine for who we used to be, what we were to each other.

I sigh. "I've had a hell of a year, Liam. If something comes up in the future, let's deal with it. But I don't want to live under the same roof just because someone might write an article about it. I don't want the awkwardness of living with my best friend-turned-lover-turned ex." My voice grows heavy. "I just want to rest."

Away from him, from temptation. From pain.

He stares at me for what feels like forever. Then, in the distance, we both hear it. The low thwap-thwap-thwap of a helicopter's blades.

"Fine."

As Liam grabs his suitcase and coat, I look out the window, watch as the helicopter lands. Snow jumps into the air.

The honeymoon is over.

I had a few days with Liam, wonderful days. That will be enough. It has to be.

CHAPTER TWENTY

Liam

Two weeks later

THE OLD HARBOR is dark. Midnight blue against the even darker backdrop of night. I can dimly make out the shape of whatever mountain is on the side of the harbor. Lights from a couple of boats glide across the water. The towers and buildings of Reykjavik cradle the harbor in a crescent. Nowhere near as tall as the buildings in New York.

I glance toward the west. Thousands of miles away, my wife may be having lunch or going for a walk in Central Park. Or regretting she ever married me.

I raise my glass to my lips and take a long, satisfying drink of my gin and tonic. The last two weeks have been hell. The helicopter ride to Akureyri had been short. Aislinn had stared out the window the whole time. I'd been too angry to try to talk with her. Her wanting to live separately had been a physical blow to my pride.

It had also just plain hurt. Putting the brakes on our physical relationship had been the right thing to do. But I never thought living in the same penthouse, a sprawl-

ing monstrosity with plenty of room, would be too painful for her.

I pause with my glass halfway to my lips. I wonder for
what feels like the umpteenth time why it was so painful.
There were times when Aislinn looked at me, the way
she would touch me, that almost made me think she felt
something more. I know she cared about me. Desired me.

Doesn't matter.

I need to stop thinking about Aislinn and focus on business. As soon as I got back to New York, my three cov-
eted clients booked meetings to officially open up their
accounts with Whitlock Investments. The office space is
leased with furniture arriving next week. My secretary is
more efficient than I am and already has a map for each
room with the furniture placement marked. And Aislinn's
PR campaign, including my blog post that went viral on
LinkedIn, has already netted me a guest spot on a morning talk show and a growing list of clients.

Including one living in Reykjavik, which is why I'm
back in Iceland just two weeks after I left.

I should be on top of the world right now. But all I can
think about is how the seat next to me shouldn't be empty.
I built my firm, worked for it with long hours and long
nights. But her recommendations have humanized my
firm, made it stand out from the rest. A detail I wouldn't
have bothered with a few months ago. Not when I had my
investment record to talk for me.

It matters now.

Someone plunks a glass down in front of me. I frown,
ready to ask the waiter to be a little more gentle. Then I
groan. "What are you doing here?"

Diana is staring at me, hands on her hips, dark eyes
narrow. "Why are you here and not home with your wife?"

"I'm here on business with my brother." I glance over her shoulder. "Where is he?"

"Parking the car. I asked for a few minutes." She sits in the chair across from me and holds up a hand to the bartender.

"Please, join me," I say sarcastically.

I don't know why she's angry. I can't believe Aislinn would have told her about what happened between us at the villa. But I can't think of another reason why Diana would be so angry.

"What happened between you and Aislinn?"

Okay, so she doesn't know. Relieved, I drain the last of my first drink and pick up the second. The bartender comes over to take Diana's order, giving me a moment to compose myself. "What are you talking about?"

"Something's happened." Her eyes widen. "The FBI? The investigation?"

I shake my head. "No. The investigation into her has been formally closed. There's not much we can do about the joint assets. But she's in the clear."

"What about Eric and Stephanie?"

I stay silent. "It's not my story to tell."

Diana's shoulders sag. "We're supposed to get together sometime soon, but…" She sighs. "I hate how distant she is."

Me, too.

I had anticipated tears when I told her we needed to stop the sexual aspect of our relationship. Tears or at the very least some sadness. God knows I didn't want to stop. Seeing her in the bed where I'd made love to her just hours ago and not touching her had been physically painful.

But she just accepted it. Accepted it and then took

things a step further by asking if we could lead separate lives.

I was surprised by how much that part of it hurt. I had enjoyed my time with Aislinn. Yes, it had been punctuated by periods of intense emotion and hard confessions. But walking out in the mornings and seeing her there, sharing meals, talking with her with the added intimacy of knowing her body just as well as I knew her mind, had made me...happy. Content.

Does it make you happy?

In the last two weeks I've gotten close to one of the biggest goals I've spent over half my life working toward. I have the money, the prestige and now the recognition.

I haven't felt happy. Not once.

No, I concede. There was one moment. Aislinn texted me to inform me she had turned down the job offer from the Foster Foundation. I was happy for her. Proud of her. And then I spent the next two days with my pulse jumping every time my phone dinged.

She hasn't texted again.

"She looked really sad."

My head snaps around. "Aislinn?" At Diana's nod, I lean in. "When did you see her?"

"Video call. Earlier today." Diana's watching me with an intensity that puts me on guard. "She told me about turning down the Foster Foundation job."

I smile slightly. "I'm proud of her."

"I am, too." Diana quirks her head to one side. "But she still looked miserable."

I look away. I've talked to Diana before about past lovers. I never did with Aislinn, though, I realize with a frown. I never confided in her the way I did Diana, never sought out her advice. "Did she say why?"

"She's recovering from 'everything.'" Diana holds her fingers up in air quotes. "But she's hiding something."

The bartender comes back and sets a glass of wine on the table.

Diana waits until he's gone before she speaks again. "You're hiding something, too."

"I'm not hiding anything," I snap.

"Are you harassing my brother, dear?" Ari walks in, dressed to kill in a black suit.

Diana's intensity evaporates as she smiles at Ari and leans in for a kiss. I look away. It's better than it was, but it's still odd to see one of my best friends kissing my big brother. "Just a little friendly questioning."

"More like an interrogation," I shoot over my shoulder.

Ari sits down across from me. It's so odd to see my eyes staring back at me. Our mother's eyes.

A fist clenches around my chest, squeezes. I never knew her. Never heard the sound of her voice, never felt her arms around me. But I miss her. I miss the woman who loved me, who gave up her life for mine.

I wish I could have known her.

This time, instead of shying away from grief, I pause. Let it in, bit by bit. But it's not just grief. There's admiration, longing, gratitude.

"I went to Goðafoss."

Ari gives me a small, sad smile. "Beautiful, isn't it?"

"Stunning."

Diana reaches over and grabs Ari's hand, squeezes it. "I wish I could have known her."

"She would have loved you." Ari leans over and kisses Diana on the forehead with casual intimacy.

It's strange seeing my brother so relaxed. The first time he was uptight, cold. Now he's relaxed. Content.

Happy.

Ari turns to me. "You said you had some business questions?"

"Yes." I gaze down at my gin and tonic. "Your company, the way you run it. How do you decide what community initiatives to invest in?"

My question surprises Ari and Diana both.

"A lot of the focuses were already established by my grandfather. But we also host community meetings and town halls at least once a year to make sure we're investing in the right things and addressing any concerns."

"I hadn't thought of that."

That approach will be a challenge in New York. There are over one million people in Manhattan alone. But it's not impossible.

"What brought this on?" Diana asks as she picks up her wineglass.

"A conversation I had with Aislinn." I swirl my drink, watch the slice of lime spin inside the glass. "I've been focused on myself for a long time. I want my company to be more than just an investment firm that helps wealthy people stay wealthy."

The thought of expanding what token gestures I'm currently doing into something that will make an impact is more exciting than any of the clients I've signed.

Aislinn was right. She had always been able to see to the heart of me.

I pause with my glass to my lips. The same is true for me. I saw all of the things she never gave herself credit for: her compassion, her wit, her passion. Yet I never allowed myself to see her as a woman. Ignored the feelings that have been there for years because I didn't think I'd ever be able to be who she needs.

But I never asked her. I never talked to her, never told her about the feelings rising to the surface. I did exactly what she accused me of; making decisions for her and taking away her choice.

"I love Aislinn." A smile spreads across my face. "I'm in love with her."

"I knew it!" Diana turns to Ari and holds out her hand. "You owe me later."

I glare at her. "You bet on me being in love with our best friend?"

"Oh please." Diana rolls her eyes. "The way the two of you were looking at each other before your wedding ceremony was hot enough to burn the greenhouse down."

"And you?" I ask, turning to Ari.

Ari holds up his hands. "I thought you might have feelings for Aislinn. But I wasn't sure how she felt about you."

The possibility that Aislinn might not feel the same way makes my chest tight.

"She does," Diana says softly. "I knew on your wedding day. I saw the way she looked at you."

My fingers tighten on the glass. "I pushed her away. I didn't think… God, I didn't think."

Diana reaches out and grabs my hand. "I did the same thing, Liam. You know Aislinn." Her eyes glint with unshed tears. "You've always known her. You never gave up on her. Don't give up on her, or yourself, now."

"I won't. But," I say with a smile, "I could use some help."

CHAPTER TWENTY-ONE

Aislinn

One week later

I STIFLE A yawn as Diana's chauffeur navigates the car down the road.

"You'll have a better view of Hvannadalshnjúkur in just a minute," Viktor, the chauffeur, says from the front row.

I glance out the window. It is impressive, a huge sprawling mountain covered in snow. Dawn is still a few minutes away, but the peak of the mountain is bathed in an orangey rose. Stunning.

And I can barely summon any emotion for it.

It's been nearly three weeks since I returned to New York and moved into the brownstone. I've seen Liam a couple of times, once for dinner with William Luther and his wife and another for a going-away party at his old firm. Each event drained me, left me feeling like a husk of myself. Holding on to Liam's arm, smiling and pretending like we're in love, is ten times harder after what we shared.

After Liam rejected it all.

Except, I remind myself as the car speeds down the road, he doesn't even know the extent of my feelings. And that is the worst part of it all. Never once in a million years did I think Liam would be attracted to me, let alone make love to me. But even after we shared our bodies and our beds, I still didn't tell him how I felt.

I gaze out over the sea, still dark just before the dawn. What if I had told him how I felt? Maybe he would have still rejected my feelings.

But maybe, after what we shared, it would have changed things for him.

Diana offered me a reprieve when she called me a couple days ago and asked me to fly out and help her look for a wedding dress. She mentioned she and Ari had grabbed drinks with Liam, but when I pressed her, she'd told me that as far as she knew Liam had concluded his business with his client.

I stare out the window. We found the dress yesterday. Diana will make a stunning bride. And, I think with a small smile, I'll get to be her maid of honor, just as she was mine. At least one dream survived.

To celebrate, Diana suggested an overnight stay in southern Iceland. I'd wanted nothing more than to just go home and curl up in bed, but I didn't have the heart to tell her no. So we drove down to Black Sand Beach, then farther on to a bed-and-breakfast near the infamous Diamond Beach. Somehow I let her talk me in to getting up before dawn to see the beach at its most glorious.

The car slows down. Viktor steers into a parking lot next to a bright blue lagoon.

Diana sits up and yawns. "Oh good!" She checks her watch. "Just a few more minutes to sunrise. Ready?"

I stifle another yawn and nod. "Sure."

We get out. It's still cold, but the wind is thankfully mild.

"Okay, Diamond Beach is—" Diana's phone rings. She glances down at the screen and frowns. "Damn. It's one of my clients from Japan." She shoots me an apologetic glance. "I'm sorry, Aislinn, I have to take this. You should go on ahead."

"I'm not going without you."

Diana shoos me. "I don't want us both missing it. I'll be right behind you."

"I'm going to stay with the car," Viktor adds. "But if you just walk across the road and then follow it down, you'll see the beach."

Disappointed and a little frustrated, I turn and start walking. The wind picks up, and I burrow my face deeper into my scarf. I'm so focused on how cold and tired I am that it takes a moment for me to realize I've reached the beach.

My jaw drops. Chunks of glittering ice cover the black pebbled beach. The pebbles give way to smooth, fine sand before it descends into the ocean. The hunks of ice come in all different shapes and sizes, from small wedges to large slabs of shimmering glacier. The sun starts to creep up above the horizon. Light shoots through the ice, turning the broken bits of glacier from white to violet, pink and orange.

I turn in a circle, trying to take everything in. I feel the same contentment, the same peace, as I felt standing on edge of the fjord watching the foxes prance across the snow.

I wish Liam was here.

The thought strikes my heart like an arrow. My eyes

well up with tears. It's so beautiful, and I'm so fortunate to be here, to be with my friend.

But I miss him. I miss him so much it hurts. Even at my lowest points, he never stopped believing in me. Even when I couldn't see what I was capable of, he always did. Because of him and his encouragement, I'm applying for jobs I never would have before. Because of him, I see the strength and courage I've developed during the dark periods in my life.

I smile through my tears. Liam helped me see the good in the bad. Helped me see I'm still there in the mess. I'm not the girl I used to be, and that's okay.

The sun rises higher. The colors fade, replaced by sunbeams that pierce the ice and turn them into sparkling diamonds. The waves fall on the beach, a gentle roar that soothes some of my pain.

I need to see Liam. I need to tell him how I feel. Then, even if our lives don't align, I'll know I gave it my all.

Someone stops next to me. Irritated at the mood being broken, I glance over my shoulder, then do a double take. My heart starts to pound.

"Liam?"

Liam

God, I missed her.

Aislinn is standing in a puffy winter jacket with a scarf wrapped around her neck, hands shoved in her pockets, a hat pulled down over her hair and her nose bright red from the wind.

She's never looked more beautiful.

"Hi."

"Um…hi." She looks around. "What are you doing here? I thought you were back in New York."

I take a step closer. Not pulling her into my arms is almost killing me. "I wanted to see you."

She cocks her head to one side. "Okay. Not that this isn't beautiful, but why not just stop by Diana and Ari's place? Or come see me back in New York?"

I've gone over this probably a hundred times over the last week. Asking myself if I was sure. Not for me, but for her. I need to be one hundred percent sure that I can stand behind everything I have to offer.

And then I smile. There's fear, yes. There will probably always be fear. But I want Aislinn, want a future with her, more than anything.

"This seemed like a more memorable place to tell you I'm in love with you."

For a moment there's nothing but the gentle roar of the ocean and the murmur of the wind.

"You're what?" Aislinn finally says.

I yank my gloves off and cup her cheeks with my hands. Her skin is cold, but I don't care. I just want to touch her. "I love you, Aislinn Knightley. I have for a long time. I was just too stupid to accept it."

She shakes her head. "This…this is crazy."

"Is it?" I lean down and kiss her forehead. "You know me better than anyone, Aislinn. And I know you. You've always been there for me. You're smart, kind, compassionate. You make me want to be a better person."

"Liam…" She tries to step back.

My heart clenches as I release her. God, am I too late? Have I hurt her too much?

"I… I feel very…strongly for you, too."

Is this what a heart attack feels like? Sharp pain stabbing over and over again as I brace myself for whatever she's going to say next?

"But I want kids." She shakes her head as tears course down her face. "I can't give that up. Not even for you."

"And I would never ask that of you." I take a step toward her, grateful when she doesn't step back. "I'm going to be honest, I'm terrified to be a father. I'm afraid I won't live up to the example my father set. I'm afraid something will happen that will rip my family apart. But," I add softly as I stop in front of her, "I realized I've been living my life in fear. I never fully let anyone in, including you and Diana."

She's watching me again with that emotion shining in her eyes. This time there's no fear, just hope as I reach out and touch her face once more.

"I'm sorry, Aislinn. I'm so sorry for always keeping you at arm's length. I can't promise I'll be perfect from now on, but damn it, I want to try. For both of us."

She swallows hard. "And kids?"

"I want a life with you, Aislinn." I lay a hand at her waist, close the distance between us as my heart pounds in my chest. "I want kids with you, whether it's kids of our own or adopting or however we create a family. I never pictured myself having kids, but when I finally stopped looking at it through a lens of fear, I realized I've wanted so many things I told myself I didn't." I press my forehead to hers. "I want a family with you, Aislinn."

She sobs my name and throws her arms around me.

I crush her to me. "God, Aislinn, I'm never going to let you go again." I slant my mouth over hers, kiss her until we're both panting and breathless.

"Did Diana help you set this up?" Aislinn asks with a laugh.

"She did. Aislinn…" I lay my forehead against hers. "I told Luther the truth about the arrangement of our marriage."

She leans back, eyes wide and luminous. "You did?"

"Yes. I told him if that meant he didn't want me as a client, so be it, but I wasn't going to live my personal life for anyone but myself." I smile. "He wasn't happy about it, but telling him I loved you and was going to do everything in my power to get you to stay mollified him."

Her eyes glint with unshed tears. "Liam… I love you."

I suck in a breath. "You do?"

"Yes." She starts to laugh. "I have for years."

I pull her against me. "Then I'd say we have a lot of time to make up for."

Her smile is brilliant. "I agree." Her expression dims. "I never thanked you."

"For what?"

"For always believing in me. For giving me grace even when I didn't think I deserved it." She smiles as she glances around the beach. "Just like Sleeping Beauty."

"Oh?"

She leans up and kisses me with a passion that rocks me to my core. "It was your kiss that brought me back to life."

I grin. "Does that make me Prince Charming? I like that a lot better than a spoiled nobleman."

She laughs. The sound fills me with a contented happiness I never let myself before. I pick her up and twirl her in a circle in the middle of Diamond Beach, laughing with her as the sun climbs higher in the sky.

I finally set her down. "I propose a change to the terms

of our agreement then. Removal of the expiration date and the no intimacy clause."

"I accept."

And we seal our new deal with a kiss.

EPILOGUE

Aislinn

One year later

"YOU LOOK SO BEAUTIFUL." Stephanie comes up behind me and lays her hands on my shoulders. Her smile is proud, motherly.

I reach up and pat her hand. "Thank you, Mom."

Stephanie's eyes glisten for a moment as she leans up and kisses my cheek. "You're welcome."

She drifts away, and I turn back to the mirror. It's not often a bride gets to wear her wedding dress twice. But Liam surprised me four months ago by dropping to one knee at the lookout point of Goðafoss and proposing a vow renewal ceremony.

Our first wedding was a little rushed, he said as he slid the stunning ruby onto my finger. *I want you to have everything you missed out on.*

At first, I'd told him it wasn't necessary. We were together. We were in love. That was enough.

But I have to admit the last few months have been fun. Finding the perfect venue, picking out invitations, perusing flower arrangements... I smile over at Stephanie as she fluffs my veil for the half dozenth time. Having people there I love.

After Liam and I reconciled, he accompanied me to Eric and Stephanie's house when we got back to New York. I sat in the living room I'd spent so much time in, my hand clenched around Liam's, and told them everything.

When I finished, there was a moment of silence.

Stephanie was shocked and heartbroken to hear about everything I'd been through. Eric sat there looking resigned, defeated.

And then he surprised us by admitting to all of it. Favoring certain government contractors who contributed to his campaign, sharing legislative information with companies to help them invest during those early years of his campaign. He also said that while Stephanie had signed off on some of the checks, they'd looked like straightforward donations. She'd had nothing to do with any of it.

I'd seen the emails, the financial records. I knew it was true. But hearing Eric admit it, while incredibly painful, had also been freeing.

Tears prick my eyes. It had also given us a new foundation, one Eric had created when he'd asked if he could hug me.

I don't deserve you as a daughter. But God, I'm going to try to be better.

He took things a step further by holding a press conference the following week. He admitted everything and told the people of New York that it would be their choice to decide whether or not to trust him again. When he won by a very slim margin, he asked me to come back and work for him.

I appreciated the gesture. But it was time to move on.

"Are you all right?"

I give Stephanie a watery smile in the mirror. "Yes. It's just…it's been a crazy year."

"It has." She reaches up and slides the clip of the veil into my hair. "But it's been a good one."

I nod. Liam's firm is growing. Luther surprised him by staying on and recommending other clients. He and his wife have become close friends. They'll be in the conservatory today watching as we renew our vows.

Liam also moved fast on the foundation. Six months after our wedding, we opened the doors of the Boundless Foundation. Liam wrote a check and stepped back, letting the board of directors and my leadership team take control of the foundation's focuses on adoption, independent living for older foster kids about to age out and foster family support.

The one thing Liam has thrown himself into has been the Carpentry School. He spends several nights a month at the school, visiting with students and even taking a few classes alongside the kids.

And our nights are spent in our new home, a condominium in Central Park South that we've made into a home.

Stephanie's phone chimes. She glances at the screen and smiles. "The pastor is ready. I'm going to do one more check, and then we should be good to go." Stephanie slips out, leaving me in the dressing room just off the conservatory.

Just over four dozen guests are seated inside the luscious New York Botanical Garden. In a few minutes, Liam and I will say our own vows.

A knock sounds on my door.

"Yes?"

I can't discern the mumbled reply from the other side, so I get up and open the door.

"Liam!" I laugh as he slips inside. "You can't see the bride in her wedding dress."

"I already have." His eyes flare as he looks me up and down. "I forgot how gorgeous you are in it."

I have zero willpower as he pulls me into his arms and kisses me.

"You do realize Diana will kill you if she finds you in here."

"She's making out with Ari down the hall, so I doubt she'll care too much."

I chuckle. "This seems…impossible."

"What?" Liam asks quietly as he traces a finger down my cheek.

"This. All this happiness."

"You deserve it," he murmurs. "You deserve everything, Aislinn."

I hesitate. Do I tell him now? Or do I wait until after the ceremony? Going with instinct, I grab his hand and guide it to my stomach, lay it flat against the slight swell beneath the waistline of my dress.

He stares at my belly for a moment before his head snaps up. "Really?"

I nod, my throat tight. "I know we just filed the papers to adopt, so maybe—"

"So maybe we'll just have two." He says it with such certainty it brings tears to my eyes.

I watch him as he stares at my stomach with a smile that tugs on my heartstrings.

"I…oh my God." His fingers tighten for a moment before he draws me into a gentle hug. "You're going to be an incredible mother."

"And you a wonderful father." I kiss him. "I love you, Liam. Always."

"Always."

* * * * *

Did Wed for the Headlines *sweep you off your feet?*
Then you're sure to love the previous instalment
in the Red-Hot Icelandic Nights duet,
Enemy in His Boardroom*!*

In the meantime, check out these other stories
from Emmy Grayson!

Prince's Forgotten Diamond
Stranded and Seduced
Deception at the Altar
Still the Greek's Wife
Pregnant Behind the Veil

Available now!

Get up to 4 Free Books!

**We'll send you 2 free books from each series you try
PLUS a free Mystery Gift.**

Both the **Harlequin Presents** and **Harlequin Medical Romance** series
feature exciting stories of passion and drama.